W9-BDC-179

Great Lengths

Sandra Diersch

James Lorimer & Company Ltd., Publishers
Toronto, 1998

© 1998 Sandra Diersch

All rights reserved. No part of this book may be reproduced or transmitted in any form or by any means, electronic or mechanical, including photocopying, or by any information storage or retrieval system, without permission in writing from the publisher.

James Lorimer & Company acknowledges the support of the Department of Canadian Heritage and the Ontario Arts Council in the development of writing and publishing in Canada. We acknowledge the support of the Canada Council for the Arts for our publishing program.

Cover illustration: Sharif Tarabay

Canadian Cataloguing in Publication Data

Diersch, Sandra
    Great lengths

(Sports stories)

ISBN 1-55028-623-4 (bound) ISBN 1-55028-622-6 (pbk.)

I. Title. II. Series: Sports stories (Toronto, Ont.).

PS8557I385G73 1998   jC813'.54   C98-930350-0
PZ7D53Gr 1998

James Lorimer & Company Ltd., Publishers
35 Britain Street
Toronto, Ontario
M5A 1R7

Distributed in the United States by: Orca Book Publishers,
P.O. Box 468
Custer, WA USA
98240-0468

Printed and bound in Canada

For Grammie.
Special thanks to Chris,
Mom and Dad,
Lezlea, Jon, Sandi,
Tina, and Sally
for all their help.

Contents

1

New Season

Jessie dove into the water, splitting the glassy surface cleanly. She pulled hard with her arms, following the pattern of the tiles below her. She loved being in the water, loved the pull of it on her body, how light it made her feel. As a small child, her parents had had to drag her from the bath, every night, wrinkled and shivering. Her mother claimed they had put her in competitive swimming because it was cheaper than installing a pool in the backyard.

The water swayed and rocked with the movement of her body and that of the other members of her swim team jumping in around her. Jessie stroked again and moved toward the surface, feeling her lungs beginning to strain. As she broke the surface, breathing hard, she was suddenly pulled under again.

Michael appeared in front of her, his short brown hair floating around his head, his blue eyes large behind his goggles. Jessie shoved him and pushed to the surface again, with Michael popping up beside her. He laughed as she fought for breath.

"What do you think you are doing, Colliard?" Jessie cried. She lunged at him and held him under the water, taking mean satisfaction from his struggles to get away.

"We're even, okay?" he said when he finally succeeded in escaping her grip. Jessie splashed water at him and moved toward the shallow end of the pool.

"What would the first day of a new season be without the ceremonial dunking?" Michael asked, winking at Cody, Katie, and Diane who were standing by the side, watching him.

"Safer, probably."

"But not nearly as much fun, trust me," Michael said with a grin.

"You love it, Jess," Cody Berenson told her, laughing. He moved out of the way as Jessie tried to smack him.

Michael looked around the pool. "Some new faces this year. Wonder what kind of competition they're going to be?"

Jessie followed his gaze as it travelled across the pool and over the deck. There were swimmers gathered around one of the team's five coaches.

"Most of them look pretty young. Watch out, here comes Tamara," Jessie said, as a girl approached them. "Hey, Tamara! You made it back for another season did you? I thought you would have given up by now; you'll never beat me, you know."

Tamara Jensen sat on the edge of the pool as she adjusted her bathing cap and goggles. "It's always nice to know some things don't change, like Jessie Cameron's ego. Don't you know by now that there is more to life than swimming?" She slipped into the lane with Jessie and Michael, cringing as the cold water hit her skin. "I wish they'd warm this pool up," she muttered.

Jessie caught Michael's eye and they started splashing Tamara, ignoring her screams.

"Enough already, I'm wet!" she cried, trying to block the water with her hands. "I see very little is going to change this season. You two are annoying as usual. Say," Tamara said, interrupting herself. Her eyes travelled down the pool deck. "Who is he?"

Jessie and Michael followed her wide-eyed stare. "Oh, he's new; just came from Calgary," Michael explained. "Troy something."

"I'll say Troy something," Tamara repeated, her eyes still on the new guy.

"What's the big deal? He's just a guy," Jessie said, impatient to start practice.

"What's the big deal? Jessie, are you blind?" Tamara asked. "He's a hunk."

Jessie looked up again as Troy lowered himself into the next lane. He disappeared under the water for a second, then came up, shaking his blond hair back from his face. He was very muscular and tanned. He caught Jessie's eye and winked at her, his eyes running quickly up and down her body. Jessie turned away, embarrassed. Tamara giggled.

"Caught ya! Isn't he something?" she hissed.

"What's a little muscle?" she whispered as their coach, Maddy, approached their lane.

"Sorry I'm late, guys," she said, crouching above them. "I had some business to take care of." She gave them their warm-up routine, and one at a time, they pushed off.

Jessie felt a little rusty as she moved through her first lengths. She could almost hear the creaks in her joints. It wouldn't take long before those were gone, it never did. This was the beginning of her sixth season with the club. She had started when she was eight, the very same day as Michael and Tamara. And they were still together.

* * *

The three hours went by quickly. Jessie could hardly believe it when Maddy called time. Jessie hauled herself out of the water, cringing slightly at the aches in her muscles.

"Overdo it?" Michael asked, falling into step beside her as they headed for the changing rooms. Jessie nodded, rubbing her arms.

"As always. I almost caught you and Cody a couple of times today," she said. Michael laughed.

"That is not likely to ever happen," he said as they grabbed their bags from the bleachers. "Don't take forever, I have to go out at seven," Michael told her and disappeared into the men's changing room.

Jessie found a shower and stood in the hot spray. It felt good; the stinging jets momentarily soothed her aches. She peeled her bathing cap off her head, slipped out of her bathing suit and closed her eyes. Around her, the voices of the other girls mixed with the sound of the water falling over her. She could hear Tamara giggling and some of the others answering her. Familiar sounds, just as the bleachy smell of chlorine was a familiar smell.

Jessie finished showering, grabbed her things, and found an empty space on a bench. The locker room was slowly emptying; only a few girls remained. Tamara grinned at Jessie in the mirror as she dried her hair.

"Some practice, eh? Maddy always keeps us hopping. I wonder why I keep coming back each year?"

"Mainly because of the guys," Jessie told her as she towelled dry. "Where else are you going to be constantly surrounded by so many jocks?"

Tamara stuck out her tongue. "Ha, ha, ha, Jessie Cameron. Ha, ha, ha," she said easily.

They finished dressing and walked out of the changing room at the same time.

"Well, I'm going to go and introduce myself to that new guy, Troy. He is too completely awesome," Tamara said, swinging her bag over her shoulder and plastering a smile across her face. "See ya later, Jess," she called back to Jessie.

Jessie shook her head and laughed. Tamara was incredible. She spotted Michael leaning against the wall and they walked out of the stuffy Aquatic Centre together. The late August evening was still warm; Jessie's wet hair felt good against her neck and shoulders.

"I can't wait until you get your licence," she said as they headed for home.

"Tell me about it. I'm so tired of having to walk to and from practice every day."

Jessie threw her bag over her shoulder. "At least it isn't very far. And we do get rides when the weather gets bad," she reminded him. Despite her hot shower, she still felt tired. Her arms and legs were aching in a nagging way. Yet the evening was so beautiful, she didn't really mind the short walk.

"I'll be glad when this first week is done. It's always so hard getting back into it," Michael said, interrupting Jessie's thoughts.

"I wish we'd never left. I ache all over and probably will for the next week. I'm so glad we start practising before school starts. At least when we go back to school in two weeks, I'll be able to walk normally! So what do you think? Any real competition in the new people?" she asked.

"Hard to say. That Troy character is fast. Knows it too."

"Tamara seems impressed, that's for sure, but then it doesn't take much with her."

Michael laughed and shook his head. "I imagine she'll have him running for the hills before too long."

"Who knows? Maybe he goes for her type: pushy and annoying," Jessie said.

"Say, wanna go to the movies this weekend?" Jessie asked as they arrived in front of her house.

"Yeah, sure. We'll have to make it a late one though, I've got stuff to do Saturday."

"Whatever. See you tomorrow," Jessie called as she headed up the driveway and into the house.

2

Siblings

Jessie stared at the page of chemistry questions and tried to make sense of them. She had read them four times already and she still wasn't getting it. In the two weeks since school had started, that had become a common occurrence. She tossed the pen down on the desk and stared at the wall of books above her. In another second, her eyes closed and all thoughts of chemistry and everything else she had to do slipped from her mind.

She was almost asleep when the door to her room swung open and her little sister, Dayna, stood there.

"What's up, twerp?" Jessie asked.

Dayna scowled. "That horrible Carla Evans told everyone at school that I cheated on the math quiz!" she cried, throwing herself down on Jessie's bed.

"How do you know she did that?" Jessie asked, coming and sitting beside her sister.

"Leanne just called to tell me. Carla told everyone! I won't be able to go to school again ever!" Dayna started crying, pushing her face into Jessie's side.

"Did you cheat?" Jessie asked. Dayna's head shot up and she glared at her sister.

"No! I'm not a cheater!"

"Good. Probably no one believes Carla anyway. Didn't you tell me she spread another rumour about someone else last week?" Jessie asked. She brushed some stray hairs from Dayna's cheek. Her face was wet with tears.

"Yeah. It wasn't true either," she said.

"There you go. So everyone probably knows Carla is a liar and no one takes her seriously. But if anyone asks, you just say, 'I don't need to cheat. I can get good marks by working hard.' And I bet they'll all believe you, really."

"Yeah, I guess you're right. Still, it hurts that some people might believe that I would cheat. Have you ever cheated, Jess?" Dayna asked, sitting up and wiping her damp face on her sleeve.

"No. If you work hard, you shouldn't need to cheat. It wouldn't make you feel very good, inside," Jessie said, thinking about it.

"Mom and Dad would kill us if they found out we were cheating on anything," Dayna said and Jessie laughed.

"I doubt it. But they would be disappointed. Are you okay now? I really need to get some work done for tomorrow." Dayna nodded and ran out the door.

The chemistry textbook was still waiting for her when she went back to her desk. The questions glared at her, daring her to answer them. This time, however, when she read them, they began to make sense. She quickly wrote out the answers and closed the book with a bang and dropped it on the floor beside her. The pile on the floor tonight was rather small, the stack on her desk still quite large. She sighed heavily and reached for her English books.

Sometimes Jessie wished she could just quit school and swim full-time. She believed that there was very little that school could do to further her career as an Olympic athlete, but her parents had just laughed when she had suggested it. She had also suggested finishing high school by correspondence, but they had laughed at that as well.

Jessie knew from talking to one of her teammates who had made the Canadian Olympic team how hard it was, how hard they worked. Jessie wasn't afraid of the work. She was only afraid of failing, of losing. In her eyes, there was no bigger failure than not coming in first. Second best didn't count, couldn't count. She couldn't remember the last time she had failed to place in the top three at a swim meet. She expected to succeed in the pool, and she did.

She was aware that her attitude bothered others, like Tamara, and even Michael at times. Tamara thought Jessie's preoccupation with winning, with swimming, was ridiculous; she'd rather be out with her friends. Jessie had little time for people who didn't take what they did seriously. Tamara had never taken her sport seriously, which was why they had never been close friends. In the long run, Jessie was sure her way was better. She intended to go a lot further than Tamara would ever go.

Two hours later, she closed her algebra book and looked with satisfaction at the pile on the floor. It was now toppling over, while her desk was empty. She rubbed her neck as she stood up. In the family room, Jessie sank onto the couch and turned the television on. In half an hour she would be sound asleep, but it was nice to relax for a few minutes.

"Are you finished your homework, Jessie?" her mom asked, coming into the room with a pile of laundry.

"Yeah. I need some help with some of the algebra questions, but I thought I'd wait until Jamie comes home and get him to help me," Jessie told her.

"I don't know when he'll be in; he had a late shift at the restaurant tonight." Jessie moved over as her mother came and sat beside her. Her mom sighed and gave Jessie a tired smile. "Sometimes I think the work never ends," she said.

Jessie grabbed some socks from the laundry basket and started sorting them. She felt slightly guilty. "I should help out a bit more, I guess."

Her mother squeezed her knee. "You do your share. I know you have a lot going on. Too much, maybe."

Jessie glanced at her mother and rummaged for another sock. "What do you mean?" she asked carefully.

"Five hours of swimming a day, six hours of school, another two or three of homework. You're only fourteen, Jess. What about your friends? You should have more free time."

Jessie put the socks on the coffee table. She had an uneasy feeling about the direction the conversation was taking. "I like what I do, Mom. I'm not unhappy being so busy," she explained.

"I've never worried about you, Jessie. Your dad and I have always known you can handle whatever you take on. I couldn't do what you do every day, but then no one is asking me to, are they?" Her mother laughed and pushed herself off the couch. She lifted the basket of folded laundry and moved toward the stairs.

"Oh, say, what was Dayna all upset about earlier? I noticed her crying, but she wouldn't tell me what was wrong."

"Someone at school is spreading a rumour that she cheated on a math test," Jessie explained. Her mother raised her eyebrows.

"Dayna doesn't need to cheat. She does just fine in math," she said.

"That's what I told her to tell anyone who asked. Besides, the little witch who is spreading the story is a known liar. Really, I'd love to spread something about her," Jessie mumbled.

"You didn't suggest that to Dayna, did you?" Her mother asked, slightly shocked.

Jessie laughed. "No, I didn't."

"Good, because Dayna would do it!" Her mother smiled as she picked up the laundry basket. "Don't stay up too much later, you look about ready to crash," she said and disappeared up the stairs.

"Hey, how's it going?" Jamie asked, thundering down the stairs a while later. Jessie looked up at him.

"How was work?" she asked. Jamie flopped down in the leather easy chair and swung his feet over the arm.

"Same as always. Hey, I stopped by your practice this afternoon on my way to work. You looked good."

"Why'd you do that? Did anyone see you?" Jessie asked, blushing.

"No, no one saw me. What if they had?"

"I don't want to have to compete for attention with the great Jamie Cameron. You're a living legend in that club. Maddy will never forgive you for leaving."

Jamie laughed. "Maddy just wanted me for herself, that's all. Who's that new guy I saw?" he asked, changing the subject.

"You mean Troy? He just came from Calgary."

"He's quite the steroid puppy, eh?" Jamie said.

"What do you mean by that?" she asked.

"Come on, the guy is what, fifteen, sixteen? Look at the size of him. You don't get muscles like that from swimming alone, my dear sister."

"You think he's taking drugs?" Jessie asked, shocked by the idea.

"Maybe not. He could be heavily into body building too. But he sure is a big sucker. Fast too. He sure seemed interested in you. He watched you all the time I was there."

"He wasn't watching me, Jamie. Don't be an idiot. Really."

"Believe what you will, Jess. But Troy was watching you. Just be careful," Jamie said.

"I don't need the lecture, or the warning, thank you very much," Jessie told him. "I'm very capable of looking after myself."

"Whatever you say," Jamie said with a shrug. He swung his legs onto the floor and pushed the chair back. He closed his eyes. "You're no ugly duckling, Jessie. Guys are going to watch you now and then."

"Shut up, Jamie. You talk too much," she told him, feeling herself blushing again at his words. "Hey, I need some help with my algebra homework. Have you got a half hour?" she asked, suddenly remembering the unfinished work upstairs. Without waiting for her brother's answer, she ran upstairs to get her books.

3

Social Life

I have never understood your fascination with chlorine and aching muscles, Jessie Cameron," Joanna grumbled. She leaned against the next locker and watched as Jessie dumped books into her backpack.

"I've been swimming the entire time you've known me Jo," Jessie reminded her. She looked through her bag quickly then slammed her locker shut and spun the lock.

"Just this once? Please, come with me," Joanna begged her voice taking on a whiney tone.

"I'm sorry. I can't," Jessie said. She wished Joanna would just drop it, but she knew that wasn't going to happen. Until Jessie walked away with Michael, Joanna would beg and plead with her to come to the mall.

"You know, you live a very one-dimensional life, Jessie The only people you know are jocks, and most of them are stuck-up — except Michael, of course. I don't know why I stay friends with you." Joanna kicked a piece of scrap paper lying on the linoleum. Jessie threw her head back and laughed.

"You stay friends with me because I'm wonderful. Really Look, I don't have anything planned for this weekend, okay?"

"What, no meet? No extra practices?" Joanna feigned surprise.

"Do you do this with Michael too? 'Cause I don't know why he keeps going out with you if you do," Jessie said.

"No. I'm sorry. Michael and I were going to get together, but why don't you come with us? I've hardly seen you since swimming started."

Michael was waiting for them outside. Jessie glanced from one friend to the other and back. "I don't know, maybe Michael doesn't want a tag-along," she said.

"I invited Jessie to come along with us on Friday," Joanna explained.

"I don't mind if you come with us. We're just going for pizza and a movie," Michael said with a shrug. "I hope we pick a better movie than the one we saw last month. That was awful."

Jessie looked from Michael to Joanna. Did she want to be a third wheel on her friends' date? "Okay, I'll come with you," she said, finally.

"Good. See you two later. I'm going to the mall!" Joanna told them and ran off in the direction of the bus stop.

Michael and Jessie went the opposite way, walking slowly along the street. Football practice was being held in the field alongside them. Jessie watched, amazed at how the players moved with all the equipment they wore. She was glad she wore only a bathing suit.

This was the end of their third week of school and practices were well under way. That initial rustiness Jessie always felt was pretty much gone; she was feeling strong and was anxious for the first meet of the season next weekend. Sometimes she couldn't believe how quickly time was passing, and how much work she had to do. She was swimming for two hours every morning, as well as the three hours each afternoon. The evenings never seemed to be long enough by the time she got home from practice and ate dinner. Sometimes she fell into bed long after the rest of her family, only to get up two hours before everyone else the next day.

Was she crazy, as Joanna thought? Or just driven? Joanna didn't understand the competitive spirit that drove Jessie and Michael and she never had. You had to work hard at anything to be the very best; swimming was no exception. Jessie was in the pool five hours a day, five days a week, and sometimes it didn't feel like enough. She couldn't afford a slip or loss of concentration. She wondered if there was any way she could squeeze more practice time into the already crowded days.

"Why so quiet?" Michael asked.

Jessie turned to look at him, slowly coming out of her thoughts. "Just thinking," she told him.

"About …?" he pushed.

"About what Joanna said. How she never sees me," Jessie said with a sigh. "We're always practising or competing, or at school, or doing homework. It doesn't leave a lot of time for other things, does it?"

"Isn't that what you want?" Michael asked. "As long as I've known you, Jessie, you've wanted to swim. Takes a lot of commitment to go the distance, to be the best."

"You sound like a commercial or something. I know all that, Michael." She shrugged. "My mom said something similar, you know, about all my time being devoted to swimming. Do you ever think about the stuff we don't have time for?" she asked.

"All the time. But we make choices, right? Any time you don't want to do it anymore, no one is going to make you."

Jessie knew he was right. She had never doubted her choices were the right ones for her, but sometimes, like when Joanna griped, or when she saw her other friends going out when she had to go to practice, then she wondered.

"I know. You're right," she said. "Too bad there aren't more hours in a day."

* * *

"Thank goodness my mom offered to drive us this morning!" Jessie said as she and Michael dashed from the Aquatic Centre on Friday morning. They dove into the warm dryness of the waiting car and instantly the windows steamed up.

"Mrs. Cameron, you are a life saver," Michael said, pulling a towel from his bag.

"No problem. I have a late meeting today. Here's your breakfast, Jess," her mother said, passing a bag over the seat.

"What movie are we seeing tonight?" Jessie asked, pawing through the bag. Her mom had packed two cereal bars, chocolate milk, a banana, and a peanut-butter sandwich. She grabbed a cereal bar and opened it.

"I don't know. Whatever you guys want," Michael told her.

"No, you choose. I hate trying to decide."

"Are you sure you wouldn't just like to choose for yourself? Anything I pick out is going to be wrong anyway. You and Joanna already have something in mind and just want to make me look stupid."

"I'm sure you don't need our help to look stupid. Hey, how'd you do on that algebra quiz? Wasn't that mean? Jamie helped me study or I never would have made it through," Jessie said. She crumpled her wrapper, shoved it into the overflowing ashtray and opened another one.

"You're a pig. Don't you ever stop eating?" Michael complained, glancing at her.

"I try not to eat while I'm swimming. Other than that, I pretty much eat all the time. I work hard, Michael. I need to keep up my energy."

Mrs. Cameron glanced at Jessie in the rearview mirror and laughed. "Michael, you have no idea. She eats more than Jamie and Dayna combined."

"Thank goodness I don't pay your grocery bill," Michael teased, shaking his head.

She ate just as much at the restaurant that night. From across the table, Michael stared at her. Jessie ignored him. It wasn't as though she had gained a pile of weight or anything.

"I don't know about *Space Camp*," Joanna grumbled, poring over the evening paper. Michael had suggested two different movies, but as he had predicted, Jessie and Joanna had shot them both down.

"It's probably pretty stupid," Jessie agreed. She wiped her fingers on her napkin and stared over Joanna's shoulder.

"I told you I didn't want to pick in the first place," he whined. The girls ignored him. Suddenly Jessie poked her finger at the paper.

"This one! This is it. *Galaxy Raiders*. It sounds like a *Star Wars* sequel or something. That's what we'll see and it starts in an hour. Perfect. Okay?" She looked around the table. Michael just blinked at her.

"You are amazing, Jess," he said.

"Yes, I am," she agreed with a grin.

Michael and Jessie were yawning when the movie let out just after eleven. Joanna looked at them and laughed. "You guys are pathetic!" she said.

"What time did you get up? Hmmm? Seven, seven-thirty? We were up and at the pool by six, swam for two hours then went to school all day," Jessie reminded her.

"Not all of us are crazy like that, Jess. Some of us appreciate sleep."

"I'd be more than happy to come and get you up so you can come with us to morning practice sometime, Jo," Michael offered.

"No thanks."

"One day we'll get you to a practice, or a meet one week-end. I thought you would have caved in by now," Jessie said as they climbed onto the waiting bus.

Joanna shook her head. "Then I'd smell as bad as you two do all the time," she said.

"Actually, we'd have to throw you in the pool for you to smell as good as we do," Michael said.

There was one light on when Jessie let herself into the house. She watched from the door as Michael and Joanna walked away, then made her way up the dark staircase, leaving the downstairs light on for Jamie. She undressed quickly, throwing her clothes onto the ever-growing pile by the closet door.

In the bathroom, she stood for a long time before the mirror, gazing at her reflection. Compared to Joanna, and even Tamara, Jessie didn't consider herself all that pretty. Joanna was beautiful, with her long, straight, blond hair, and brown eyes. She was tall and slender and, despite the fact that she hated exercise with a passion, she was very fit. Of course, Jessie reminded herself, Joanna didn't eat much. She had only had one piece of pizza at dinner.

Did boys prefer the blond cover-girl looks that Joanna had over dark-haired girls? she wondered. Jessie had dark hair, chestnut they called it, and it got a bit unruly if she let it grow too far past her shoulders. Since she spent so much of her time in a swimming pool, she had always kept it shoulder length, like it was now. Her eyes were dark too, and her eyebrows. She was short, only 5′ 3", where Joanna was 5′ 7". She wasn't that bad looking, was she? The mirror didn't answer, so Jessie turned out the bathroom light and went to bed.

4

Anchor

Gather round people, I have your meet schedules. Please be on time Saturday and Sunday! There are going to be a lot of clubs there and warm-up will be crowded. I don't mind if you buzz off when you've finished racing in the morning, but you'd better be back for warm-up for finals if you've qualified! Last meet a few of you were late," Maddy said as she moved swiftly up and down the deck handing out the meet schedules.

"She burns more energy moving around the deck than we do in the pool five hours a day," Michael whispered to Jessie.

"Really. I don't know how she can be so pumped all the time. I'd be exhausted," she added, watching her coach. Maddy, Madeline for those people brave enough, had been coaching the senior swimmers in the club for three years now. Jessie couldn't remember her ever missing a practice or swim meet in all that time. She was always on deck ready to encourage and cajole reluctant athletes, her long, dark braid swinging across her back in time to her hurried steps.

Sometimes Jessie heard the rhythmic slap-slap of Maddy's sandals on the deck as she swam, and she knew her coach was somewhere above her, watching her like a hawk. No one had ever seen her in anything but her sandals, shorts, and T-shirt. Occasionally she wore trackpants, but not very often.

"Here you go, Jess," Maddy said, breaking into Jessie's thoughts. Jessie blushed, glad her coach couldn't read her mind.

"Thanks," she mumbled and glanced quickly through the schedule for her name. She was entered to swim six individual events and two relays over the two days.

"Can I get a ride? My parents can't come until lunchtime," she said to Michael.

"No problem."

"Busy weekend, eh? Eight events this time. I really need to work on a couple of them too. I only qualified for one event at Nationals last summer," Jessie said, reading down her events sheet.

"You gotta stay focused, Jess. It's tough at Nationals, there's way too much going on and so much pressure. You'll do better this year," Michael told her.

"Second time lucky? I still have to make my times at the qualifying meets though," Jessie reminded him with a sigh.

Michael and Jessie arrived at the pool just before eight, Saturday morning. Quickly they found their team's spot in the bleachers and dumped their bags.

"Lots of yawning this morning people. What'd you do, party all night?" Maddy asked from her place at the top of the bleachers. She always said it gave her the best view of everything. It seemed to work too, because she always knew exactly where everyone was and what they were doing. Jessie glanced around the group of athletes quickly, checking to see who was there. After so many years of competition, Jessie knew almost everyone. They all swam against each other over and over through the year.

She finally noticed that everyone was moving to the pool for warm-up and she stood up to join them. Jessie slid into the pool, cringing at the coolness of the water. It was barely eight o'clock, Saturday morning. Too early really, to be doing this.

But Jessie knew she would rather be in the pool than any-where else. The first meet of the season was always exciting. She started off nice and easy, letting her arms and legs warm-up slowly. She took her time and swam the sixteen lengths Maddy expected of them for warm-up, four of each stroke. Then she climbed out and headed for the bleachers.

"Hey, Jessie," Troy said, sliding onto the seat beside her.

"Good morning," she said, looking up at him. He looked good in the club's turquoise-and-white warm-up suit.

"So, is this a good club?" he asked, glancing around the pool.

"Not bad. They usually hold the first meet every year. Lots of clubs enter, you know, to get things going. You'll probably run into some stiff competition from the team from Duncan."

"They're good, eh? Well, no problem. Local meets don't phase me too much anymore. There was a time when I would have been puking in the john right about now," Troy told her.

"I know what you mean. I still get butterflies before each event. I think it's healthy. You know, keeps you competitive." She fingered her turquoise racing cap, running her fingers over the smooth rubber. When she looked up again, she caught Troy's eye and blushed.

"I understand you're the anchor for the girls' relays," he said.

"Yes, I am," she told him matter-of-factly.

"I'm looking forward to seeing you swim in competition. From what I've seen at practice, you're very good." His praise brought another blush to Jessie's cheeks.

"Thank you," she managed to mumble. He had been watching her! Just like Jamie had said. She didn't quite know what to make of that.

Once the day's events got underway, everything moved very quickly. Jessie swam her first two events, winning them easily. Her times were good, although not her best efforts.

"It's the first meet of the season, Jess," Maddy reminded her, patting her on the shoulder. "We've only been practising a few weeks."

Still, Jessie thought she should have done better. She pulled her T-shirt over her head, wincing as she extended her right shoulder. Slowly she moved the arm in circles, stretching the muscles, but that same pain shot through her shoulder each time. Great, she thought. What have I done to it? She continued to stretch it and gradually the pain subsided to a dull ache.

Her parents and Dayna arrived just before lunch and came to sit with the club.

"I caught that last performance, Jess," her mother said, sitting down beside her. She pulled a tube of deep heating rub from her purse and opened it. "You looked strong. Did you improve your time?" she asked.

Jessie turned so her back was to her mother and let her rub the hot cream into her shoulders and back. The muscle she had strained earlier had been feeling okay, but it felt good to have it massaged.

"Yeah, I did okay. Maggie Collins beat me, but only by a tenth of a second or something. We've been going back and forth all day, as usual," she said, closing her eyes.

"I missed doing this, do you know that?" her mom said with a laugh. "I used to do a bunch of you. At the end of a weekend my hands would stink to high heaven. I remember how you and Michael would fight over who got to be first. Michael won't let me do this anymore. He says he'd rather have a sixteen-year-old doing it than his best friend's mother." Her mom found the sore spot and Jessie squirmed slightly.

"Remember the first meet you were entered in? How the coach pulled you out of the water because you were practically drowning? I'll never forget how mortified you were. I was relieved. Another second longer and I would have been down there pulling you out myself."

"That coach was an idiot. She should never have had me swimming four lengths in the first place. Do you remember how she used to throw kickboards at us during practice when she wanted to get our attention?" Jessie asked.

"I remember her; she got fired. She always hit the wrong person," Michael added, joining them.

"How does that feel?" Mrs. Cameron asked, wiping her hands on a towel. Jessie moved her shoulders around and nodded. It was still sore, but the massage had helped.

"Good, thanks. Hey, you guys, they've got our event up on the board. We should get going," she called to Tamara, Diane, and Katie. She stood up, reached for her goggles and bathing cap, and moved toward the pool deck. The others followed her.

"What a madhouse," Katie said as they collected in the marshalling area.

"Really. I'm glad I'm not claustrophobic," Jessie said, laughing. There seemed to be a sea of bathing suits and white officials' uniforms. The chattering of twenty-four girls rose around her, familiar and comforting. No matter how many times she swam, Jessie always enjoyed it. She glanced around the pool area. It was a small aquatic centre as far as they went. Teams that couldn't fit in the three sets of bleachers along the one wall were huddled on the pool deck in groups, trying to keep out of the way of busy officials. The noise of chatter and cheering and whistles blowing rose and fell continuously, echoing off the water and the high ceilings. It was damp and hot and noisy and crowded and smelled overwhelmingly of chlorine. Jessie took it all in.

In an alcove at the side of the pool, benches had been set up for the swimmers to sit on while they waited. The marshall sat at his table handing out time cards and arguing with coaches and athletes over missed events and incomplete cards. Since this was a relay event, there were even more people milling around than usual.

Jessie stood at the edge of the pool with her teammates, urging each swimmer on. She eyed the competition carefully, keeping a watchful eye on who was swimming where on the other teams. When Diane climbed out of the pool, she bent over to catch her breath.

"Where are we?" she asked.

"Third now. Come on, Tamara! Pour it on!" she screamed. By the time Tamara had finished her fourth length, they had slipped to fourth position.

"Don't hold anything back, Katie," she said as Katie climbed onto the starting block.

Katie nodded, as she shook out her arms and rolled her head, loosening her muscles. She stepped to the edge of the block, then launched herself out over the water. Tamara climbed out of the water and grabbed her towel. Jessie stretched as she cheered Katie on, carefully working the sore shoulder, loosening it up.

Katie swam hard, but they were still sitting in third when she started her fourth length. Jessie climbed on the block and curled her fingers around the edge. She had been in this position before and she could handle it. As Katie's hands hit the wall beneath her, Jessie dove off the block. She sailed out over the water, hit it kicking, and started stroking hard. The water was choppy from the movement of so many people and her body felt tossed. She kept her head down and focused all her energy on winning. She knew there were two girls some- where in front of her and she had four lengths in which to pass them.

Jessie flipped at the wall and headed back the way she had just come. Her heart pounded, her lungs burned, but she paid no attention. She swam as though being chased by demons. She turned at the wall for the third time and headed down the pool on her last lap. Every tiny piece of her burned with exertion, yet she found just a bit more. Just a little, but it was enough.

Jessie slammed her hand into the wall and looked up into the screaming faces of her teammates. She grinned as she slapped the water.

"Way to go, Jessie!" they screamed, grabbing at her, pulling her out of the water to slap her on the back. She let herself be drawn into the circle of bodies, smiling and congratulating them in return.

5

Good Form

Let's get going on warm-up, people!" Maddy called to the swimmers assembled around her on the pool deck Monday morning. Jessie stretched her right arm around in circles, warming-up the muscles as she listened. She had iced her shoulder after the weekend meet and had stretched it slowly and carefully, but it was still bothering her.

Around her, everyone else was stretching and warming-up as well. We look like a bunch of windmills, Jessie thought as she looked around. Across the deck, she spotted Troy. He flexed the muscles in his arms and chest as he stretched. He looks like a Greek god, like Adonis or someone, she thought. His hair was bleached to a light blond and curled tightly on his head. His back was wide, and heavily muscled. He caught her eye and winked. Jessie blushed and turned quickly away.

What did she think she was doing? It irritated her that she thought about Troy at strange times during the day, not just at practice. What was it about him that made her keep noticing him? She had been surrounded by muscular, scantily clad guys for years and had never cared. She wanted Troy to be no different, but it seemed that he was.

Jessie had no chance to think about Troy again during the practice. Maddy had them working so hard, Jessie was sure she would pass out.

"Not fast enough on the fast lengths, people! We had some good swimming this past weekend, but that's no reason to slow down now. No slackers allowed!" Maddy yelled, walking up and down the deck, her whistle swinging from her neck. Jessie sagged against the wall and wondered if she could just sleep for a minute or two, if anyone would notice.

"Sometimes I really despise Maddy," Tamara hissed as they waited for Maddy to stop her tirade.

"Really," Jessie agreed.

"Why do we keep listening to her? That's what I don't understand. She's just a little tyrant," Cody said under his breath, glaring at Maddy's retreating back.

"Full of her own power, that's all," Michael added. They kept one eye on Maddy as she paced up and down the deck.

"We should put itching powder in her gym bag, or we could not show up for practice. With no one to boss around, she wouldn't be happy at all," Tamara said, glaring at the coach's back.

"Tamara, we come to swim hard. Really," Jessie reminded her, but Tamara only waved her comment away.

"I heard something interesting," Tamara whispered, changing the subject.

"You're always hearing something, Tam," Michael told her.

"I heard, if you're interested at all, that some swimmers from a team in Calgary tested positive for steroids. You two probably swam against them last year at Nationals," she said, nodding at Michael and Cody, then she stood back to watch their faces as they took in her news.

"Bull, Tamara! Where'd you hear that nonsense?"

"Hide your head in the sand if you want, Jessie, but it's true. Maddy was talking about it earlier. It seems our own little sport is not as pure as we would like to believe."

"I heard it too," Cody added. "It's happening in lots of clubs. Maybe even this one."

Jessie glanced at Cody and then back at Tamara. The two of them were always so concerned with gossip and rumours, always eager to share some little secret, especially if it discredited someone they didn't like. She didn't believe a word of it.

"Why would anyone want to wreck their bodies like that? Who was it? Do you know any names?" Michael asked.

"No, I didn't get any names, but I tell you, if I ever found out about someone on this team using steroids, I'd be in Maddy's office so fast. I think it stinks," Tamara said fiercely.

"It could just be rumour," Jessie said. "Honestly, you two are willing to believe absolutely anything."

"Okay, people! Down to the deep end. We're going to work on some sprints. Those of you who tend to die doing this, stay at the back of the lines," Maddy called and they all climbed out.

Jessie made her way to the deep end and found a place behind Michael. She glanced over and found she had lined up opposite Tamara.

"Gonna whip your sorry butt, Cameron," Tamara whispered as they stepped to the edge. Jessie adjusted her goggles and ignored Tamara.

Jessie beat her easily on the first three lengths they did, but then Maddy called breast stroke and Jessie's heart sank. She didn't stand a chance against Tamara in breast; it was the girl's best stroke and Jessie's worst. Sure enough, when they reached the other end, Tamara was half an arm in front of Jessie. She turned and grinned.

"Gotta keep you in line," she said as she climbed out of the water. "Can't let you think you're Club Queen all the time."

"One sprint does not a queen make," Michael quipped.

"Tamara is just tired of being Club Jester, that's all," Jessie said.

Jessie walked back to the deep end behind Michael and Cody, watching the way their bare feet splashed the pools of water on the deck. She was getting tired and her shoulder was hurting. She glanced at the clock; half an hour to go. This afternoon was feeling like an eternity. Cody's voice broke into her meandering thoughts suddenly, startling her.

"Did you see how he dove in just ahead of the whistle?" she heard Cody say to Michael.

"He always does that," Michael replied. "Some kind of Calgary technique or something. Of course, he thinks he's just faster than us, when really he just cheats."

Cody laughed and shook his head. Behind them, Jessie frowned. They had to be talking about Troy.

"Ever since the first day of practice, I couldn't stand him," Cody said. "Life around here used to have some rules, you know?"

"Yeah," agreed Michael as they fell into line behind the others.

Jessie closed her eyes and took a deep breath while she waited for her turn again. Michael's conversation with Cody stayed with her, though, like an itch that wouldn't go away. She had never realized before that Michael and Cody could be jealous of another swimmer.

"How's it going?"

Jessie looked up, startled, to see Troy standing beside her. "Oh, I'm fine. Tired now. I'm not the best sprinter in the world."

"It does take a lot of energy. But you looked pretty good — good form, nice technique," he told her and Jessie blushed. She was uncomfortably aware of how close Troy was standing.

"Thanks, I guess," she said and stepped away as Maddy blew her whistle.

"What was that all about?" Tamara asked, appearing at Jessie's side.

Jessie blushed furiously again and shook her head. "Nothing," she said.

"He watches you all the time, Jess," Tamara said, moving in close. "He likes you. I can tell."

"Tamara, please. You are being ridiculous. Troy was just being friendly," Jessie told her firmly and stepped to the edge of the pool.

6

Best Friends

If Jessie thought that was the end of the conversation, she was mistaken. Tamara started up again as they headed for the changing room at the end of practice. Tamara grinned wickedly at Jessie as she turned on a shower.

"Looks like a little romance is blossoming beneath our very noses," she said.

"Please, Tamara, would you just drop it? Really, you're being annoying now," Jessie told her, turning away. Tamara wasn't to be put off.

"What's wrong, Jess?" Tamara asked. "I know you like Troy, I've caught you watching him too. What's the big deal?"

Jessie closed her eyes and tried to hide under the spray of the shower. Tamara was like a dog with a bone, she wouldn't give it up. Why was the girl always aware of who was watching who? Didn't she swim during practice? Jessie almost asked her, but then thought better of it. She turned off the water and moved to a bench.

"I bet he asks you out soon. What will you tell him? Will you go?" Tamara asked, dropping her bag down beside Jessie's.

Jessie ignored her and concentrated harder on towelling off and getting dressed. Maybe, if she just kept quiet, Tamara would get bored and go away.

"Will you promise to tell me all the details?"

"Tamara, stop already! Troy does not like me, I don't like him. No one is asking anyone else out and if they ever did, I wouldn't tell you anything. Now would you please just leave me alone so I can get out of here?" Jessie snapped at last, embarrassed and tired. Tamara took a step back and her face fell slightly. She shrugged and moved away, leaving Jessie to finish dressing in peace.

Michael was waiting in his usual place in the lobby when Jessie came out a few minutes later. They pushed through the front doors and walked out into the cool October morning.

"It's getting cold," Michael observed, pulling his zipper up higher on his coat. Jessie didn't answer. "What's up with you?" Michael asked, nudging her with his elbow.

"Oh, Tamara was being irritating, that's all." She shrugged it off. "I'm a bit tired too."

"You know what Tamara was going on about today? About steroids in some other club?" Michael said.

"Yeah, so? You don't really believe her do you?" Jessie asked.

Michael looked over at her. His face was serious. "It happened in a club in Calgary, Troy's old club," he said. "I asked Cody about it."

"Do you always believe everything Cody tells you? It's a pile of crap, Michael, really."

"It happened, Jessie. A bunch of people on the team Troy swam with in Calgary were suspended from the sport. There was an investigation and everything."

"Swimmers don't use drugs. That only happens in track and field and weightlifting. You and Tamara have got your stories wrong somehow," she insisted, refusing to believe his words.

"Anyone can take drugs if they think it will help them to win. Swimming is no exception."

"It has nothing to do with us, with our club," Jessie said, confused.

"Troy left the club in Calgary just after all this happened," he said simply.

Jessie made a snorting sound. "Give me a break, Michael Colliard. Are you trying to tell me that Troy left Calgary because he was involved in all of that? Get real. He would have tested positive and he wouldn't be able to swim here either. You are cracked. Really."

Michael shrugged. "I don't know why he left Calgary, no one does. Anyway, it's something to think about." They had arrived at the school.

"I have no intention of thinking about it any more. I'll see you later," Jessie said and headed for her locker.

* * *

"How's it going, Jess?" Troy asked as they left the pool later that week.

"Fine. Good," Jessie said, suddenly very interested in the strap on her goggles. She loosened one side and then the other, stalling.

"You looked real good today, strong," Troy said, touching her elbow with his fingertips. Jessie forced herself to look up at him.

"Thanks," she said shyly. They had stopped walking and stood facing each other on the busy deck, forcing the other swimmers to move around them to get to the changing rooms.

"Listen, Jess, I was wondering if you would be interested in going out with me this weekend," he said.

Jessie could hear her heart pounding in her chest, and her mouth felt dry. "Sure, I guess that would be okay. Thanks," she managed to say at last.

"Great! Saturday night, okay? I'll call you with the details?"

Jessie could only nod, feeling suddenly tongue-tied. They both turned as Michael came up to them. Jessie resisted the urge to put a hand to her flaming cheeks.

"Hey, Mike. How's it going?" Troy asked.

"Fine thanks. Could you hurry, Jessie? I have to get home quickly today," Michael said.

"Yeah, I'm coming," Jessie told him. Troy looked at Michael and then at Jessie.

"Hey, am I stepping on toes here or something?" Troy asked.

"No, not at all. I'll talk to you later." She smiled and ran for the changing room.

"What did he want?" Michael hissed at her later as they left the building together.

"He was making conversation, chatting," she said. She paused for a split second. "He asked me to go out with him Saturday night," she finally told him. He was very quiet for a second.

"Are you going?" Michael wanted to know.

"Yes, I am." I am going out with Troy on Saturday night, she said again to herself and smiled. Beside her, Michael stared straight ahead.

"I don't like that guy. He's not what he seems," Michael told her at last. "He's always strutting around the changing room and the pool deck like he's some kind of a god or something. I don't trust him. He probably was involved with those guys in Calgary. I don't think you should get mixed up with him."

"Get off it, Michael. You're just jealous because he's faster than you are," Jessie teased but Michael swung around and glared at her, his eyes furious.

"I am not jealous of anyone, especially not Troy Aitken. He's bad news and I don't think you should be going out with him," he said through clenched teeth. Jessie felt her cheeks redden with anger.

"You are not my brother or my father," she snapped. "And you have no right to tell me who I can spend time with or anything else, Michael Colliard. I would appreciate it if you would remember that in future." They glared at each other, standing in the middle of the parking lot. After a long heavy silence, Michael broke away and walked off.

"We're going to be late for school if you don't come on," he called back to her and slowly Jessie followed.

The silence on their walk to school was overwhelming but Jessie did nothing to try and end it. Michael was out of line and she wasn't about to start apologizing like she had done something wrong by talking to Troy. If she did that, Michael would think he could tell her what to do all the time. Instead, she let her mind drift to other things and ignored him.

Michael disappeared as soon as they got to the high school. He wasn't at their lockers when she arrived either. Jessie put her books away and hung up her jacket. She found the books she needed for her morning classes then closed the locker door. She could count on one hand the few fights she and Michael had had in all the years they'd been friends. When they argued, she felt sick.

"Hey, what's with Michael? He barely said hello just now when I passed him," Joanna said, appearing at Jessie's side.

"We had a big fight. He's ticked off because Troy asked me out on a date and I said I'd go," she said, wincing as Joanna punched her in the arm.

"Way to go Jess! I knew it! Don't worry about Michael. He likes to pull this jealous big brother crap once in a while. He'll come 'round eventually," she said.

"Yeah, I know. I'm sure it will blow over by this afternoon."

Jessie could tell the minute she saw him that afternoon that Michael was still in his mood. She walked along in silence for a block or two and then she'd had enough.

"I'm going to slap you in a second Michael if you don't cut the silent treatment. I didn't do anything wrong, and you know it, so stop acting like a jealous boyfriend," she told him. For a second she thought he was going to tell her to go ahead and smack him, but then he looked over at her and half-heartedly smiled.

"Okay, okay. I overreacted. I'm sorry. The guy just rubs me the wrong way. I don't trust him."

"Well, it's not like he is proposing marriage or anything. He just wants to go out with me. And really, Michael, since you have no proof that Troy has done anything wrong, you should lay off."

7

Troy

"Well, who is this guy, Jessie?" Her father asked when Jessie told him about her date. She could feel Jamie behind her, staring at her.

"He came from Alberta in August. He's a year older than me. He's a perfectly nice guy, Dad. There's no reason to worry. I'll be fine."

Mr. Cameron met Jamie's eye over Jessie's head and she tensed, waiting for Jamie to spoil everything with his suspicions.

"Do you know this boy?" he asked. There was a pause before Jamie answered.

"No. He joined after I quit," Jamie said.

"Your mother and I are going out Saturday night, Jessie. We would really rather have a chance to meet this Troy before you go out with him," her father said, looking from Jamie to Jessie.

"I'll be home, Dad. I'll check him out for you," Jamie told him and Jessie felt her stomach fall. Great. She would have had a better chance with her father. Jamie would have Troy running from the house.

"I guess that would be fine, if you don't mind, Jamie. Don't stay out all night though, Jessie. I think eleven-thirty is plenty late enough." Jessie nodded and glared at her brother as she left the room.

* * *

When Troy rang the bell Saturday night, Jessie ran to answer it, narrowly beating Jamie to the door.

"Hi, Troy. I'm ready to go," she said, trying to push past her brother, but Jamie was already offering Troy his hand.

"I'm Jessie's older brother, Jamie," he said pleasantly.

"Nice to meet you, Jamie."

"So, Jessie tells me you're new to Vancouver. You swam in Calgary?" Jamie asked, leaning against the door.

Jessie tried not to look impatient as they talked. She played with the strap of her purse, wishing Jamie would hurry up and let them go. She couldn't believe how thorough Jamie was being. Her father would have been a whole lot easier to deal with.

"Yeah, but I'm pretty happy with Vancouver so far," Troy said, winking at Jessie. "I understand you swam with the club?"

"Ten years, start to finish," Jamie told him. "Decided there were other things in life besides a swimming pool. Unlike Jessie here. She still hasn't figured that out." They laughed together while Jessie stood fuming.

"Do you mind if we get going, Jamie?" she hissed. Annoyingly, Jamie rested a hand on her shoulder and continued with the questions.

"Did you know any of those guys who got nailed in Calgary last year for steroids?" Jamie asked casually.

"Jamie!" Jessie cried.

"Yeah, I knew some of the guys," Troy said, shaking his head. "They've all been suspended. I guess there was quite the investigation. I left just as it was getting started."

"Steroids can really mess up a person's life. But I guess sometimes the temptation can be pretty strong, eh? I know there were times when I wished I could get a bit of a boost, just to get me over that last hump."

"I know what that's like. Last summer, at the Nationals, there were some guys, you know, you just had to wonder. I started lifting weights instead. No point in wrecking a perfectly good swim career, right?" They laughed together and Jamie stood back.

"Well, you guys have a good time," he said and let them go.

"Sorry about that. He can be a bit annoying," Jessie said when the door was closed behind them.

"No problem. I take it your parents aren't home tonight?" he asked as they walked to the bus stop.

"No, they're out playing bridge or something like that. Although, my father was ready to cancel so he could stay home and meet you. Jamie finally convinced him that he would handle it."

"Be thankful you have people in your life who care about you," he said. Jessie looked over at him, surprised at the sadness in his voice.

"I am. Do your parents not care much about what you do?" she asked.

"I live with my dad. Mom is in Calgary. He doesn't really pay too much attention to what I'm up to. He didn't even come to the Nationals last year."

"That's too bad, Troy." She thought of her sometimes overprotective parents. They drove her crazy with their questions and concerns, but they had always supported her swimming. They came to her meets, helped out with her club, drove her back and forth to practices. When she needed them, they were there.

"That must be rough," she said.

"I'm used to it," Troy told her, shrugging his shoulders. "He's this self-employed insurance guy. You know the type.

He's never home, always out with clients or at meetings, or whatever. He was like that when he and Mom were married." Troy shrugged again and kicked at a pop can lying on the sidewalk.

"Is that why they got a divorce?" Jessie asked.

"Partly, I guess. They stopped getting along a long time before he started in with the insurance thing. He's only been doing that for about five years."

"That's lousy, Troy," Jessie told him. She felt a deep sense of relief that her parents were together, in one house, and happy.

"Yeah, well. Let's talk about something else, okay?" Troy suggested and the subject was dropped.

* * *

"This is shaping up to be a great year for me. I almost wish the Olympic tryouts were this season," Troy said as they walked out of the theatre after the movie. "My times are right on. I'm on top of things. I think this new team will be good for me, push me harder than Calgary — not that they weren't great athletes."

Jessie laughed and nodded her head. "I know what you mean. It's amazing isn't it? I mean, there are other meets, but the Olympics are the most important. To me anyway," she said softly. Troy reached for her hand and squeezed it.

"I know. You'll go far, Jessie," he told her. Jessie smiled in the dark, feeling she could do absolutely anything.

Troy held her hand as they walked from the bus stop to Jessie's house. It was warm and strong and Jessie liked it being there. "I had a really good time tonight, Troy," she said. "Thank you for inviting me."

"I was kind of afraid you would say no. I mean, I wasn't sure about Michael and all."

"Michael and I are just good friends. He's dating my friend Joanna as a matter-of-fact," Jessie told him. They had arrived at her front door and stood awkwardly together in the soft glow of the porch light.

"Then maybe we could go out again sometime?" Troy asked, sounding a little unsure.

"I'd like that." She tipped her face up to smile at him and found his there, waiting for hers. His kiss was soft and gentle and quick.

"Good night, Jessie," he said and ran down the driveway.

* * *

Jessie slept late Sunday morning then hung around the house in her bathrobe for a long time, reading the morning paper, eating, watching television. She worked on a couple of assignments for a while, but she couldn't keep her attention on them and finally gave up. She wanted to talk to Joanna about her date, but Joanna was at church and Jessie knew she wouldn't be home until after lunch.

"So the steroid puppy from Calgary got you home safe and sound, did he?" Jamie asked, standing in the doorway to Jessie's room. Jessie scowled at him from her desk.

"Please don't call him that. His name is Troy."

"Troy. Sorry! Did you have a good time?" Jamie asked, his tone slightly less sarcastic. Jessie, longing to tell someone about her date, nodded.

"Yes. He's very nice, Jamie, very polite and interested in what I have to say. The restaurant was really good and the movie was funny."

"You know no one will ever be good enough for my little sis," Jamie told her. "Just be careful."

"Jamie, if you are so certain he's bad news, why didn't you tell Dad the other night? You could have," Jessie asked.

She had been curious, grateful, but curious ever since that night.

Jamie met her eyes and looked at her steadily for a second, then he shrugged. "Dad would have freaked and you would never have spoken to me again. Since I don't have any proof, just suspicion, it seemed better to leave things alone. Like I said, be careful."

"I'm always careful. Wanna hear about the movie? You would have liked it," Jessie said, dropping the subject.

"Stop! I don't think I want to hear the intimate details of my baby sister's date. Save it for Joanna, okay? I've got to get to work," Jamie said and ran down the stairs.

Jessie listened to him leave the house. She found some sweats at the bottom of her closet and put them on, then brushed her hair and made her bed. Then she sat down at her desk to tackle some more of her homework.

By the time Joanna arrived at the door just after lunch, Jessie had waded through most of the work. She was glad to put it away and forget about it for a while.

"So, tell me everything. How was it? Was he wonderful, does he want to see you again?" Joanna asked, throwing herself on Jessie's bed.

"It was pretty nice, really. We talked about swimming mostly, surprise, surprise. But he told me all about Calgary, about his coaches, and the International meets he's been to. He's swam all over the world. It's incredible."

"I think you like Troy because of his swimming ability more than anything," Joanna teased.

Jessie stuck her tongue out at her friend. "Like you and Michael? You just wanted a jock boyfriend, right?" she teased back. Joanna laughed and threw a pillow at her, knocking Jessie over.

"He's really nice, Jo, very sweet."

"Did he kiss you?" Joanna wanted to know.

"Yeah, he did," Jessie told her, blushing.

"Is that it? No juicy details?" Joanna asked. Jessie shook her head, her face still red. "I'll just have to use my imagination then, I guess," Joanna said, grabbing a pillow and smothering it with kisses. "Oh Troy, Troy, you're such a hunk," she moaned. Jessie grabbed another pillow and started beating her with it.

8

Sidelined

"Kick, Jessie. Come on, use your legs! You're not even trying!" Maddy screamed from somewhere above her head. Jessie tried to concentrate on her stroke, on the endless corrections Maddy was making. Kick harder, pull further, straighten this, bend that, breathe, don't breathe, push, pull, on and on. Jessie couldn't do anything right today.

"What was that?" Maddy yelled at her as Jessie came to a stop at the end of the pool. "Your stroke is really off today Jessie, you're not even trying." What was Maddy's problem? Jessie wondered, keeping her eyes on the water. The words ran into one another as Maddy went on and on. "Okay! Everyone, 4x200 IM on three-thirty, all out! GO!" she screamed finally, and the lead swimmers pushed off.

Jessie adjusted her goggles and pushed off just behind Cody and Michael. She kept her legs tightly together and kicked like a dolphin under the water, finally coming up for air, her arms swinging in wide arcs over her head. Butterfly was the most difficult of all the strokes and Jessie's favourite. On good days, anyway. Today she felt like lead weights had been attached to her hands. She could barely get her arms out over the surface of the water and she felt winded. On top of all that, her shoulder was killing her. Ever since the October meet, it had been aching and she had been forced to ice it before and after almost every practice.

What was wrong with her today? She wondered, touching and turning at the wall. She had no energy, no strength, and she had been bothered by a cough for the last couple of days. Her stroke was off, bringing Maddy's wrath down on her almost the entire practice. To add insult to injury, Jessie felt Tamara's fingers brushing at her toes. Jessie dug down deep and found more energy. She pulled away from Tamara's touch.

"You guys forget how to swim today?" Maddy asked, her voice cutting the air with sarcasm. "I'm going to add another 200 to the end of this if you don't improve," she went on. "Jessie, I've seen ten-year-olds with a better stroke than you're showing today. Get with it!" She moved away again.

"Don't sweat it, Jess," Troy whispered, leaning across the lane marker toward her. His sympathy nearly drove Jessie mad, but she just smiled.

"I'm fine, really," she said. Jessie rinsed her goggles, snapped them back over her head and started off again. She wanted to go home, crawl into bed, and stay there.

Somehow she made it through the practice. She took her time in the shower, and dressed slowly. She was so tired! Her throat seemed to be worse too, and it hurt to cough. She pushed all thoughts of illness away though. She had no time for it. There were meets to prepare for and mid-terms approaching.

"You feeling okay, Jess?" Troy asked when she joined him in the lobby after practice.

"All right. I've had better practices, though. That's for sure," she told him, stifling the annoying cough. He put an arm around her as they swung through the large glass doors and walked out into the cool autumn air just ahead of Michael.

"How're you doing, Jess?" Michael asked, coming up beside her.

"I've been better. I'm sure I'll be okay by tomorrow, though. Probably just need a good night's sleep, really."

"Well, see you later then," he said, without a word to Troy, and moved away. Jessie watched him go in silence, furious, but helpless.

Jessie went to bed right after dinner, ignoring the stack of books piled on her desk, and the laundry waiting to be folded. She was sure that if she just got a good night's sleep, she'd be fine in the morning. After all, she was incredibly healthy, seldom even got a cold, let alone the flu.

The next morning she felt no better, but kept it to herself, determined not to give in to illness. She allowed herself to relax the usual pace she set for herself at practice, but by the end of the week she could barely make it through the three hours in one piece.

"Jess, you don't sound very healthy. Why don't you climb out and get dressed? You should get that cough checked out." Maddy knelt down at the side of the pool on Thursday.

"I don't know what's wrong with me. I can't seem to shake this thing," Jessie said. She pulled her goggles off her head and looked up at her coach.

"No fight? No argument? You must be sick," Maddy said.

"I always hate to admit when someone else is right, but this time you and my mother are. I think I'll go and have a soak in the whirlpool. Maybe that will help my chest." And my shoulder, she thought.

"Go to the doctor, Jessie. It could be serious," Maddy told her.

* * *

The doctor's office was busy and they had to wait for almost half an hour before the receptionist showed them into an examining room.

"I haven't been in here for ages," Jessie said, looking around. "This was probably the same magazine he had then." She picked it up and showed her mother.

"I'm sure he has more important things to think about than the age of his magazines," her mother said.

"You'd think that would be a concern, considering the length of time he makes us wait," Jessie commented, then turned to see Dr. Edwards coming through the door. She smiled sheepishly.

"Making you wait am I?" he asked, sitting on his stool.

What was it about doctors? Jessie wondered, watching him read through her thin file. They all looked older than everyone else. Dr. Edwards, with his wire-rimmed glasses and neatly trimmed brown hair and mustache, could have been thirty or fifty. Everything about him was tidy: his shirt and tie, his trousers and black shoes, and the white lab coat. The stethoscope that hung around his neck tucked neatly into the pocket of his coat beside a neat row of pens. Jessie hid a smile and looked away.

"So," he asked finally, looking up at her. "What seems to be the problem?"

"I can't get rid of this cough I've had for a week now. It's interferring with swim practice," Jessie explained. She cringed at the coldness of the stethoscope as he placed it against her chest and back. She breathed deeply when he asked her to, stopping to cough once or twice. When he was finished, he sat down again and wrote on her chart for a few seconds.

"Well? Absolutely nothing, right? A stronger cough medicine?" Jessie asked, impatient at his silence.

"No, unfortunately it isn't nothing, Jessie. You've got bronchitis," Dr. Edwards said, turning to look at both of them. Jessie felt her heart sink. "I'm afraid you're going to be sidelined for a few weeks."

* * *

"I guess we know why you've been off lately, eh?" Michael said when Jessie called him the next morning. She closed her eyes and leaned against the wall for support. It seemed the doctor's words had given her body permission to completely give in to the illness. She felt worse today than she had all week.

"I guess I won't be at practice for a while," she croaked. "My mother has me under house arrest. Keep me up-to-date, though, okay? Hopefully, I'll be back in a couple of weeks. Soon as the warden lets me out."

"I'll call you after practice this afternoon. Take care," he said and hung up. Jessie climbed back into bed and fell asleep.

"You asleep, Jess?" Dayna whispered later that afternoon. Jessie blinked at her, trying to focus.

"Yeah, mostly," she said.

Dayna came in and sat beside her on the bed. "You feeling better yet?" she asked, smoothing the blankets.

"No, not really. But I will. How was school today. How was that horrible Carla?" she asked.

"Just as horrible. Today she got sent to the office for picking on a little kid. I was kind of glad," Dayna admitted.

"Really. I always like it when Maddy picks on Tamara; she drives me so crazy."

"I almost forgot!" Dayna cried. "Someone just phoned for you. Mom took a message."

"Who was it?" Jessie asked, sitting up.

"I don't know. Do you want me to get the piece of paper?" Dayna asked. Jessie nodded then leaned against the pillows and closed her eyes. She could guess who it was. In a second Dayna was back with the message.

"It's from your boyfriend, Troy," Dayna said, batting her eyelashes and dragging out Troy's name suggestively.

"I'll call him later, if I don't die first. He's not my boyfriend; we're just dating," Jessie said.

"Hey, I thought you said you didn't have time for a boyfriend, he'd just get in the way of swimming."

"It's not the same when he swims too, Dayna," Jessie told her. "It would be hard to date someone who wasn't swimming, 'cause I'm always at the pool. But Troy is there too, so it's easier."

"I think it's just because he's really hot looking and you couldn't help yourself!"

"Dayna Cameron! Shut up and get out of here," Jessie snapped. Dayna dropped the message on the bedside table and slipped out of the room.

9

Time Passing

"Geez, I hope they let you back in a pool soon," Jamie said, moving aside as the TV guide Jessie had just thrown sailed past him. "You're an absolute bag."

"Leave me alone, Jamie Cameron! Get out of my face," Jessie snapped, scowling furiously. She started to cough and couldn't stop. Jamie watched her from the far side of the room, his eyes concerned, but Jessie could concentrate only on coughing, on trying to catch her breath. Stupid chest! She was sick of it! Sick of being tired and worn out and bored! She wanted to go back to the pool, back to her friends, even back to school.

"Are you all right?" her brother asked. Jessie nodded, still unable to speak. Finally the fit subsided and she could breathe more normally. She lay back against the easy chair and closed her eyes.

"I'm fine. Could you please just leave me? I would really rather be alone," she asked.

"Yeah, whatever. I'll be upstairs if you need anything." Jamie left the room and Jessie was alone.

Usually Jessie didn't mind if her brother was around. They had always gotten along fairly well, but Jamie in a teasing mood was more than Jessie could handle today. She'd been home from school and practices for a week. The bronchitis was slow to respond to the antibiotics Dr. Edwards had given her, and she was close to breaking point.

Jessie turned the TV on and absently flipped through the channels. Talk shows and soap operas blared out at her, but nothing really held her attention. She had homework to take care of, but she didn't feel like tackling it. Her mother had gone to the school and requested assignments for her, so she wouldn't be too far behind when she got back to class. It was hard, though, to focus on assignments and projects when she wasn't actually going to the class. She had started reading the new novel for English, and had actually worked through a lot of the algebra, but that was as far as she had gone.

She must have fallen asleep, because when she next opened her eyes, some new program was on the television and it was getting dark outside the patio doors. The phone rang next to her chair and she reached over to answer it.

"Hi, it's me," Troy said on the other end. She smiled. He had been faithful about phoning every day before practice started and had come by in the evening twice so far.

"Hi. How was school?" she asked.

"Same as always. How're you feeling today? Any better?"

"About the same. Will you come over tonight?" she asked.

"You bet. I'll bring a pizza," Troy promised.

"Sure. Are you at the pool already?" Jessie wanted to know. She could picture the movements of just about everyone: The steady stream of swimmers through the front doors, into the changing rooms, out onto the deck.

"Yeah, in the lobby. Listen, Jess, I better go. I'll see you tonight, okay? Take it easy. Save some energy for me. I'll bring a movie to go with the pizza," Troy said.

"See you later," Jessie said and hung up. She stretched and reached for the remote control. The phone rang again as she was folding the blanket.

"Michael. What a surprise," she said, sitting down again. "Aren't you at practice?" she asked.

"Yeah, in the office. Just wondered how you were feeling," he said.

"Not a lot better," Jessie told him. "I just had a call from Troy."

"Yeah, I saw him on the phone in the lobby. Well, I guess I'd better go. See ya 'round," Michael said and the line went dead.

Jessie sat staring at the phone, frowning. What was his problem? she wondered. He was acting so weird these days, ever since she had started seeing Troy. With a shrug, Jessie stood up and headed for the stairs. She was too tired and feeling too lousy to wrestle with the problem right now.

Jessie showered and fixed her "sick hair" as she called it. She put real clothes on; jeans and one of her father's shirts. She looked at herself in the mirror and shrugged. She was pale and her skin was blotchy, but she didn't care. Despite her nap, she still felt lousy and her chest was tight and painful.

"You sure you feel up to company?" her dad asked as she came downstairs to the kitchen. Dinner was on the table and her family were gathered around, waiting for her. Jessie slipped into a chair and took a piece of bread from the basket.

"I'll be okay. I had a bit of a nap this afternoon. Troy won't stay late."

"Make sure he doesn't, Jess. You're not well, remember," her dad reminded her.

"Really? I hadn't noticed," she said.

"She'd better go back to the pool soon or I may do her in," Jamie said. "She tried to kill me this afternoon."

Her father looked at her, his eyebrows raised. "How serious was the attempt?" he asked.

Dayna and Jessie giggled, sneaking looks at Jamie. "Not too serious; he was being annoying," Jessie explained. She picked at the bread, putting small pieces in her mouth at a time.

"Ah, yes. The annoying James Cameron. What are you doing this evening annoying James Cameron?"

"I'm staying here to chaperon Jessie and her friend," he said. Jessie blushed and kicked at her brother under the table.

"Leave your sister alone, Jamie," their mother said mildly.

Jamie looked at Jessie. "But Mom, someone has to protect her honour," he said.

"Jessie is capable of protecting herself, Jamie. Come on you two," Mrs. Cameron said, indicating to Dayna and her husband. "We have to get going or we'll be late for the movie."

"You come downstairs even once tonight, Jamie," Jessie hissed as the others left the table. "And I will make sure you regret it for a very long time." Jamie laughed as he stood up and took his plate to the counter.

"Don't worry little sis. I won't interrupt. If you need a hand, though, just yell. I'm not going out tonight," he told her.

10

The Return

W hat's this?" Jessie asked, as a small package landed in her lap. Troy grinned at her.

"To celebrate your return to the pool," he whispered. A smile crossed Jessie's face and she picked up the wrapped package. She had been gone for more than three weeks all together. It was the middle of December now and if she thought about it, Jessie got very anxious about all the time she had lost. She opened the box carefully and found a delicate gold bracelet nestled in the cotton. Lifting it out, she saw the charm dangling: a swimmer posed to dive.

"I guess technically it's a diver, but it could be a swimmer," Troy explained, sitting down beside her on the bleacher. Around them, their teammates talked and moved about on the deck, waiting for afternoon practice to start. Jessie smiled up at Troy and then looked again at the bracelet.

"This really wasn't necessary Troy," she said, placing it back in the box carefully and putting on the lid. "I mean, it's no big deal."

"Of course it's a big deal. I missed you," Troy told her and leaned in to kiss her. Blushing, Jessie looked around the pool to see if anyone had noticed, but no one was paying any attention to them.

"I'll have to put it in my locker. Or maybe I should give it to Maddy to look after for me. She could put it in the office during practice." Jessie stood up quickly, suddenly over-whelmed.

"Maddy," Jessie said, poking her head into the office. Her coach looked up with a smile. "Do you think I could leave this with you during practice?" she asked.

"What is it?" Maddy asked. Jessie lifted the lid of the box and pulled out the bracelet. Maddy's eyes widened.

"Troy?" she asked.

"Yeah. To celebrate coming back to practice."

"Wow. He's pretty generous," Maddy said, simply. "It's good to have you back. We missed you while you were away. I guess you're completely better now?" Maddy asked.

"My mother wouldn't let me even say the word 'pool' until Dr. Edwards had given me the okay. I don't think she even believed him. I don't dare get a tickle in my throat or she'll have me back in bed again. She insisted I miss this morning's practice to get a little extra rest. It's so good to be back!"

"Well, don't overdo it on the first day, okay?" Maddy moved away down the length of the deck. The other coaches joined her.

"Well," Troy asked, coming up beside her. "Did she ooh and aah?"

"A little. I still can't believe you did that. It wasn't necessary at all," Jessie told him.

"It was terribly necessary," he said with a smile.

"Hit the pool!" Maddy called suddenly, into the warm air. Jessie slipped her goggles on and jumped into the pool.

Jessie had known that, after being away sick for so long, it would take her a while to get back to her old level of ability. She took it easy as she warmed-up, reminding herself not to be concerned that Tamara automatically went ahead of her, or even that Katie did as well. She tried not to let it bother her when Michael and Cody lapped her. She had promised to take it easy this first day and she intended to keep her promise. But when, half-way through the practice, Tamara came up from behind and then went past her, Jessie was mortified.

By the end of the practice, she was exhausted. Even taking it easy, the practice had felt like more than she could handle. She rested her head on the tiles and closed her eyes.

"You okay, Jess?" Michael whispered near her ear. She nodded her head without lifting it. "Tough practice today, but tomorrow will be better."

"Can't be much worse," she mumbled against the tiles.

"Hey, you okay, Jessie?" Troy asked, coming up behind her. Jessie felt Michael stiffen. She raised her head and looked at both of them.

"Yes, I'm fine. Just a bit tired," she said. Troy draped an arm over her shoulder.

"We'll have you whipping everyone's butt again in no time, won't we, Mike?" he asked, grinning at Michael.

"I'm not doing anything with you," Michael snapped. He pulled his goggles off his head and glared at Troy.

"Hey, what's with the tone?" Troy asked. "It was just a comment."

"Why don't you just leave Jessie alone? She doesn't need your kind of help, none of us does."

"Michael," Jessie interrupted, raising her hand.

"No, Jess, it's time Wonder Boy here heard this. We're all a bit sick of your high and mighty attitude, Aitken," Michael continued. "You think you're so incredible because you turn a few heads and impress a few people. I see through you, though, that's the thing. I know all this is a crock, even if Jessie is too blind to see what's going on."

"You are way out of line, Mike," Troy said finally, his face flushed. He moved away from Jessie toward Michael, his size more noticeable the closer they stood to one another. "I'm not doing anything but swim hard and have a few kicks with Jess.

I don't think you want to be making accusations you can't back up."

"Come on, you guys," Jessie said finally, resting a hand on Troy's arm. "Maddy is coming over. Let's just get going okay?"

"This is far from over, Aitken. Remember that. I have my eye on you," Michael said and climbed out of the pool.

* * *

Jessie was staring off into space Thursday evening, when her mother stopped at her bedroom door. She blinked and smiled. "Hey," she said.

"You were lost in thought," her mother said with a smile. "But I have a feeling it wasn't over algebra."

Jessie sighed and shook her head. "No."

"Is something wrong, Jess? I've noticed the last couple of days, since you returned to practice, that you've been preoccupied."

"Yeah, I guess I have," Jessie admitted.

"Everything all right with swimming? You aren't feeling sick again are you?" her mother asked, concerned.

"No, nothing like that. It's just," Jessie began, "well, it's just Michael. I don't know what's wrong with him. He's being very stupid these days."

Mrs. Cameron came into the room and sat on the end of the bed. "Stupid how?" she asked.

Jessie sighed again and told her the whole story, right from the first rumours of steroid abuse in the Calgary club. When she finished, she looked at her mother and shrugged. "He says he doesn't trust Troy, but he won't say what it is he doesn't trust. And then the other day at practice he started accusing him again."

"That's a big issue, Jess," her mother agreed. "The thing is, sweetie, that sometimes your friends aren't going to like each other. Sometimes, and I know you don't want to hear this, we just have to resign ourselves to it and work around it. It could be that Michael is jealous of Troy. Jealous of his speed and his obvious ability, but also jealous because Troy has replaced him in your thoughts and affections."

"But he hasn't!" Jessie objected. "I still like Michael as much as ever and besides, he has Joanna. I was never jealous of him having a girlfriend."

"I don't know about that. The thing is, Jess, that you don't need Michael as much now because you have Troy and Troy should be important because he is your boyfriend. Your first. You've had time to get accustomed to Michael and Joanna seeing each other, but this is new to Michael."

"I guess I see your point," Jessie said slowly. "So what can I do? I mean, they practically snarl at each other any time they meet up and Michael won't even talk to me half the time. It's really driving me crazy."

"I bet it is. I think, though, that you are just going to have to let time take care of things. You can't force Michael to like Troy and you aren't going to give up Troy to please Michael. I think that eventually Michael will come around and if he doesn't, well, we can cross that bridge when we get there, right?" Mrs. Cameron said. She stood up and stretched. "You should get to bed, it's late and you've had a long day." She kissed Jessie's forehead and left the room.

Alone, Jessie thought about her mother's words for a long time, puzzling them over. It wasn't the solution she was looking for, but a tiny part of her knew she had no choice. The problem was Michael's, not hers and she couldn't solve it for him.

11

From Bad to Worse

The sadness crept over Jessie slowly, so slowly that at first she was unaware that anything was really different. Long after she should have been back at the top of her performance, she was dragging and sluggish. Her turns were clumsy and slow, her starts were weak, her strokes were mediocre, and her shoulder bothered her constantly. At the end of practice, Jessie was dragging herself out of the pool and falling asleep before she finished her homework. They had had lots of extra practices and strength training over the Christmas holidays, but even that wasn't any help.

One afternoon, near the end of January, Maddy called her into the office. Jessie leaned against the door and eyed her coach.

"What's up?" she asked.

"I wanted to talk to you privately, before I handed these out," Maddy told her, waving a stack of papers. Jessie frowned, unsure what Maddy was getting at. "I have the schedules for the next meet, the one this weekend," she continued.

"And so? Am I not swimming?" she asked, prepared to fight that. She had swam in only three meets since the start of the season and she was impatient to get back.

"No, you're swimming. You've missed a lot of practice since November, Jessie. I've been watching you in the last few weeks and I can see how hard you're trying," Maddy said and paused. She looked at her hands, at the papers she held in them. Jessie followed Maddy's glance and the fear that had already started building inside her, increased.

"What is it you're trying so hard to tell me, Maddy?" she asked, her voice low. Maddy looked up and offered Jessie a small smile.

"You've been working really hard, Jess, but you're off. Your speed is off, your strokes are off. I've been watching and thinking about it for a while. I've noticed you favouring your right shoulder for a while now too," Maddy said slowly.

Jessie looked at her coach. She knew Maddy wanted to help, but she had an irrational fear that if she admitted that her shoulder was bothering her, she'd get yanked from the pool and she was desperate to avoid that.

"It's bothering you, isn't it? Has been for a while I suspect. I know you've been icing it, stretching it longer than the left side. 'Fess up, Jess. I can help."

"I strained it back in the fall at one of the meets. It isn't that bad, no big deal," Jessie finally admitted, her stomach churning.

Maddy nodded. "I don't imagine you've been to the doctor about it, or for physio. I'd like you to start going and I'd like you to keep up the ice. I'd also like to have you do some stroke work, one-on-one, two or three times a week. Darren has agreed to work with you. I think, and he agrees with me, that part of the problem is that you've been sick. You were sick for nearly a month, and maybe that has somehow affected you, thrown you off. Plus you've had some changes in your personal life, too, and that can have an effect."

"Maddy, I'd really appreciate it if you'd get to the point. I know there's more," Jessie said finally, wanting to get it all over with.

"I'm moving you out of anchor position on the relays. I want you to swim the backstroke in the medley and to swim third in the freestyle. I'm only doing this to take some of the pressure off you, give you a chance to concentrate more on your personal events."

Jessie stared hard at Maddy, taking in the words. She knew, before she asked, who had replaced her. "Who is going to swim anchor?" she asked, her voice a near whisper. Before Maddy spoke, Jessie knew what name she was going to say.

"Tamara," Maddy said at last.

The anger that churned inside Jessie rose like bile in her throat. She wanted to scream and yell, to have a fit right there in the office, to hit something. She squeezed her hand around her goggles, felt the plastic crack beneath her fingers.

"I'd like you to start today with Darren, for the first half-hour, okay? In the diving tank. And Jess," Maddy said, stretching out a hand to touch Jessie's shoulder, "this isn't a punishment. We want you back to top form. It's important to all of us that you do well. We all want you to qualify for Nationals again this year."

Jessie moved out of the office, away from Maddy's words. The roaring in her ears was louder than the noise of her teammates gathered on the bleachers. She walked past their curious eyes to the diving tank where Darren, the "stroke doctor" as he was affectionately known around the club, was waiting for her. It never occurred to her not to do as she was asked. She had always listened to her coaches. In fact, she wasn't even all that concerned about the extra help with Darren. It was losing her position as anchor on the relays that stabbed, like a knife, deep inside her.

The changing room was mostly deserted by the time Jessie got there at the end of practice. She was glad because she was terribly afraid she would cry if she had to talk to anyone. It had taken a lot for her to work through the three hours without falling apart. Every time Jessie even glanced at Tamara, she felt worse. She had purposely stayed in the pool after Maddy let them go so she wouldn't have to talk to anyone.

There was no one waiting for her in the lobby and she frowned as she pushed through the heavy front doors and out into the dark January evening. It had rained most of the day and the pavement glistened eerily in the light of the street lamps. There were few cars in the parking lot and she frowned again as she looked around for Michael or Troy. She didn't like walking home by herself, not when it was dark.

A scuffling sound caught her attention and she turned, her heart beating faster. Voices rose and fell in the silence and with a shock, Jessie recognized Troy's. "Troy? What's going on? What are you doing?" she called, moving toward the voices.

She moved around the corner of the building and stopped, stunned. Troy and Michael faced each other, bodies poised to attack. Their breath swirled around them in the cool air and she could hear them breathing heavily. "Troy? Michael? What's going on?" she asked again, approaching them slowly.

"Your friend here is a lunatic, Jess," Troy called to her, never taking his eyes from Michael. "He's trying to kill me."

"Michael? What are you doing?"

"I told you and told you this guy was no good, Jessie, and you wouldn't believe me," Michael said. "He's going to drag you down with him if you don't watch it."

Suddenly, from nowhere, Michael's fist flew toward Troy's face. Troy saw it coming and ducked aside, spinning around to face Michael again. "Back off, Colliard!" he yelled. "You're an idiot."

"At least I'm not a druggie! And I don't go around corrupting other swimmers!"

"You have no proof that I use drugs. Do you always believe every rumour that floats your way? Huh? I'm faster than you 'cause I train hard and don't waste my time worrying about what everyone else is doing," Troy said, circling Michael as he spoke.

Jessie's heart was beating fiercely and she gripped her swim bag as tightly as she could. She was terrified they would hurt each other and longed for someone to come along and help. There was no way she was leaving the two of them alone.

"Troy doesn't use steroids, Michael. He's not corrupting me, he's not doing anything to anyone. Why won't you just believe us?" she begged. "Please, Michael, stop this. Someone is going to get hurt!"

Michael ignored her plea and lunged suddenly at Troy. Troy grabbed him and spun him into a headlock, holding him firmly. Jessie ran toward them. "Let him go! Troy, please, let him go," she cried, her face wet with tears.

"I'm not doing anything of the sort until he promises to stay away from me," Troy told her, holding the struggling Michael tighter.

"Michael! Promise him. Just promise him and let's go home. Please, Michael, this is all so stupid."

"All right! I'll back off," Michael agreed finally and Troy let go, pushing Michael roughly away from him.

Jessie rubbed her face with her jacket sleeve and ran a hand through her still damp hair. Her whole world was spinning around uncontrollably. Troy handed her her swim bag and she took it, looking at him sadly. Michael had grabbed his bag and was almost out of sight now.

"Let's go home," Troy said quietly and took her hand. Jessie checked for Michael again but couldn't see him. Why did she have to choose between the two of them? Why, why, why, why? The word bounced around in her head, making her dizzy, but leaving her no closer to an answer.

12

Strong Medicine

The meet was a bust. The extra work she had done with Darren for the three days before the meet, as well as the physio appointments for her shoulder, might as well not have happened. She couldn't seem to get on top of anything, especially the relay. Gathered with Tamara, Katie, and Diane before the first relay, Jessie had swallowed hard and forced herself to take the backseat, to let Tamara do what Jessie had always done. She nodded at the right moments, kept a smile plastered on her face, and told herself to work for the good of the team and not only for herself.

Her start was sloppy and she knew it. Jessie's foot slipped from the block as she dove in. She hit the water awkwardly, pushing her goggles off her eyes just enough that water started dripping in. Concentrate Jessie, she told herself. Think only of now. The voice in her head spoke constantly as she moved through her first two laps. Her first turn was good and so was her second length, but she misjudged the amount of space she had in her second turn and when she flipped her legs over, her heel caught the edge of the pool deck. She winced and tears came to her eyes, but she pushed the pain from her mind.

She felt her shoulder give part way through her fourth lap and she couldn't move her arm without it hurting. She finished her four lengths in fifth place.

"Don't worry about it, Jess," Katie whispered to her as she grabbed her towel. "We all have days. We'll catch up."

It didn't help Jessie at all that they did catch up. In the end, thanks to Tamara's effort, they came in second. Their time was the worst the four of them had ever swam in the relay. Jessie turned away from the others, ashamed.

Back in the bleachers with the rest of the team, Jessie wanted to hide. She couldn't remember the last time she had performed so poorly in a swim meet. No, she could. The very first meet she had ever been in, when her coach had pulled her from the pool in disgrace. This was worse. Then she had been eight years old, had been swimming only a month and a half. Now she was nearly fifteen and had been swimming for more than six years. Jessie knew better.

"Get ice on that shoulder," Maddy said, coming to sit beside her. She looked at her for a long second. "I'm wondering if I should scratch you from the rest of the meet. I can tell it's hurting you a lot," she said.

"No! Maddy, please! I need this meet. I'll keep it iced until the next event, okay?" Jessie begged. After a long pause, Maddy shrugged and nodded.

"Fine, but concentrate, Jessie, focus. I know how much the relay upset you, but we've talked about it, right? We're working on the problem and we're going to get you back on top. We have to work together though, so don't do anything foolish."

There were no bright spots in the weekend for Jessie. They won the IM relay, but Jessie knew it had nothing to do with her. At the end of her four lengths, they were sitting third. Once again, Tamara managed to pull them up. Jessie was so disheartened, she couldn't even dislike Tamara for doing what Jessie had always done. To make things worse, her disastrous performances had pulled her times below the level required for the Nationals. There was only one more qualifying meet that season.

Jessie wished desperately that she could talk it all through with Michael. He had always helped her see things clearly, but ever since his blow up with Troy, things had been horrible between them. He refused to take back what he had said, or to apologize. He was being stubborn and unreasonable and she couldn't talk to him, not about anything. When she tried to get him to tell her what was going on he only told her she was blind and heading for trouble. She was beginning to realize that he didn't understand her anymore.

* * *

Troy sat back on the couch in the family room and looked at Jessie, his eyes serious. "What's wrong, Jess?" he asked. The evening was not going well. Jessie knew it was her fault, that Troy was probably ready to go home, but she couldn't help it.

"Nothing, really," she said, trying to smile.

"You think I haven't noticed? You've been miserable for weeks, even worse since that meet last weekend. You feeling okay?" he asked.

"I feel fine. Just a bit down, I guess. Do you want to go home? I don't blame you if you do," Jessie said, tears welling behind her eyes.

"I don't want to go home, Jess. I want you to talk to me. What is going on? You've been off for weeks. I keep waiting for you to tell me what's up, but you never do. Don't you trust me? Don't you know I want to help if I can?" As he spoke, Troy moved over beside Jessie, and pulled her close to him. Jessie buried her face in his shirt.

"I can't swim any more, Troy," she confessed. It took her several seconds to get up the nerve to speak again. When she did her voice was soft and hesitant.

"This whole season has just been a waste of time. I should be back on top by now. I'm over the bronchitis and my shoulder is no big deal. But no. All the extra work, all the physio, none of it is doing anything!" Jessie moved away from Troy and glared at him as though he were the cause of her trouble. "Why can't I swim anymore? Why do I feel like I'm pushing through mud every time I get in the pool? I was worse than a beginner at that meet."

"Jessie, hold on," Troy said, stopping her flow of words with his hand. "This happens to everyone at some point. You'll work through it."

"Everything I worked for is slipping away," Jessie argued, feeling tears prickle behind her eyes again. She blinked them away quickly.

"No, it isn't. Look, two years ago I had a rough year too. My parents had split and Dad had moved here. I cracked a bone in my foot playing street hockey. I didn't swim for nearly a month and when I did I was pretty pathetic. But I worked through it. It wasn't my greatest season, but I survived. And so will you. I'll help you," Troy said and squeezed her hand.

"How can you help me?" she asked, wanting to know.

"There are things we can do, stuff you can take," Troy said casually, lifting his broad, muscular shoulders as he spoke.

Jessie looked at him silently. Somewhere deep inside, the old rumour she had heard slowly woke. She had never believed Michael's accusation that Troy used steroids, but what if she had been wrong? Wasn't that what he was offering her? She wasn't all that sure what steroids did, except that they made a person stronger and faster, and what Jessie wanted more than anything was to be faster. Faster than she was now, but faster than she had been before, too. Was that what Troy was offering?

She looked at him more carefully. Was her boyfriend using steroids? What if he got caught? What if he gave some to her and she got caught? Her whole career could go up in smoke. Wouldn't that be much worse than a bad season?

What if she didn't get caught? What if they helped get her back on track? She could stop any time, couldn't she? Jessie held her hands to her head, suddenly tired. Could she cheat? She had been brought up to be honest and play fair. But if they could help her, who would it hurt really? The thoughts spun around in her head. She was tired and disheartened and slow, so slow.

"Are there side effects?" she asked finally, not brave enough to look at him.

"Side effects? To vitamin supplements?" Troy asked, sounding confused.

"Vitamins?" Jessie echoed, looking up at him.

"Yeah. I found a great health food store downtown that has a really good selection," Troy explained, then his face grew serious and he frowned at her. "What did you think I was talking about?" he asked.

"I wasn't sure," Jessie said quickly, but Troy shook his head.

"No, you thought I was talking about steroids. Jessie! Do you really think I take drugs?" he cried, jumping to his feet.

Jessie had never seen him so angry, not even when he and Michael had been fighting one another. He was hurt, too.

"I can't believe you! I thought you were my friend!" he said, not even trying to keep his voice down. "I really thought you were different from the others. Even if Michael and you are pretty tight, I thought you believed me, Jess."

Jessie shook her head. "I did! I do believe you, really. But everything is so lousy and I can't swim anymore! And you're having such an excellent season. You've made all your times,

you're having the best season of your life. I just, I hoped … "
Jessie faltered.

She didn't really know what she hoped or thought. She just knew she couldn't deal with the heavy feeling of failure that hung over her like a cloud. Tears ran down her cheeks as she looked across the room at Troy. She was half afraid he was going to leave, but she wasn't sure what to do to make him stay. "I'm sorry, Troy, I really am. I don't believe you use drugs. I never did. I'm just so frustrated and confused. When you said stuff," she paused and wiped at her eyes. "I just assumed you were talking about steroids. I never even thought of vitamins."

There was a deep silence in the room when Jessie stopped speaking. She could hear the beating of her own heart and Troy's breathing. He hadn't moved from where he stood.

"I really am terribly sorry for thinking such a thing. Will you still help me?" she asked.

Troy stared at her for a minute before he answered. "You don't want to go there, Jess, not steroids. They're bad news," he told her, his voice serious.

"But nothing's helping! Not extra help, not physio, nothing. I can't stand losing, Troy, especially against Tamara Jensen."

"Then we'll just have to work together to get you beating Tamara, okay? I'll help you all the way. We have three weeks until the last qualifier, and I know you can do it. Right?" Troy asked.

Jessie looked up at him, her face damp with tears. At last, reluctantly, she nodded.

13

Stamina

W hat's going on, Jessie?" Katie asked. She was leaning against the edge of the pool, her arms folded across her chest.

"What do you mean?" Jessie asked, trying to appear innocent.

"You know what I mean. Why do you keep adding to the sets?" Katie asked, not fooled by the act. The others had come to the wall and were gathered around, obviously interested in Jessie's answer as well.

Jessie looked at them, trying to make up her mind. Should she tell them? She wasn't a hundred percent certain they'd understand. "I'm trying to get over this slump I've been in," she confessed at last. "I'm just swimming a bit more than Maddy tells us to, that's all."

Several pairs of goggle-encased eyes looked back at her, but no one said anything. Finally Diane asked, "Is it helping?"

Jessie breathed out slowly. "It's only been a few days but I think so, a little anyway," she said.

"Did Troy help you with this?" someone asked.

Jessie turned and found Troy, Michael, Cody, and the others in the next lane listening as well. She smiled at him as she nodded. "Yeah, it was his idea actually," she said. Michael and Cody looked at each other then Michael made a rude noise and turned away. Jessie felt her smile slip, but she cleared her throat and stood up a little straighter. "I want to make my times at the qualifier next month," she told them. "Hopefully, this extra work will give me the help I need."

"Good luck," Tamara said, as Maddy descended upon them. "Does she know?" Tamara hissed.

"Yeah, I told her Monday," Jessie whispered back and Tamara nodded.

Maddy gave them their next set and they all pushed off. Jessie smiled to herself as she pounded through the water. She had been afraid they wouldn't understand, that they would block her efforts, but everyone, everyone but Michael anyway, had been okay with it.

After the first few sets on Monday morning, Maddy had called Jessie out of the water and demanded to know what was going on. "I'm not blind, Jess, I can see you're increasing the lengths I give you, taking less rest. What gives?" she asked.

"I have to make my qualifying times at the meet in three weeks, Maddy," Jessie told her honestly. "I'm just pushing myself harder."

Maddy looked at her for a minute, a small frown on her face. "I'm paid to set up challenging practices for all my athletes, especially my good athletes," she said slowly. "I'm not sure I like being second guessed on what is best for you. I also don't want a useless swimmer. What about your shoulder?"

"My shoulder is a lot better lately, actually. I'm down to one physio a week now and it doesn't hurt after practice as much as before. Look, Maddy," Jessie said, looking directly at her coach, "I have to make Nationals this year. I'm not trying to second guess you or anything. I just want to get back on top of my game. Can't we make a deal?" she asked.

"I'm listening," Maddy said.

"Well, what if I keep doing what I'm doing, just resting a little less and tacking on an extra set at the end whenever I can, and you watch me and make sure I'm not overdoing it. Please?"

"I'm really not happy with this, Jess," Maddy told her, holding up a hand to stop Jessie's objection. "But I'm willing to let you go with it for a while. You aren't to give up your stroke work with Darren, nor are you to come sneaking into the pool on weekends or any other times. No weird diets, no visits to the gym. You can do the strength-training routines we follow over the holidays. That's it. I want you in bed at a reasonable hour every night and if I hear that your school work is suffering in any way, or if your parents start complaining, it stops. Got it?"

Jessie grinned. "You bet. And thank you Maddy. I won't let you down," she promised and hopped back into the pool.

It hadn't been easy, but Jessie was determined that it would work. Working so hard helped her keep her mind from other, troubling things. Michael's reaction didn't surprise her. He barely spoke to her these days anyway, except to tell her she was crazy. Even Joanna had tried to reason with him, but she'd had no more success than Jessie. Jessie made herself stay focused on the meet at the end of March. That was all she could afford to concern herself with.

"Hey, Jess, how're you doing?" Troy asked, interrupting her thoughts.

"Tired, but okay," she told him with a smile. He had been very encouraging and supportive, helping her as much as he could, just as he had promised he would.

"Almost done for today. Then we'll find a pizza, a big one, with lots of mushrooms on it, okay?" he offered and Jessie nodded her agreement.

* * *

There was a strange buzz on the pool deck the next afternoon when Jessie came out of the changing room. Small groups of swimmers huddled together, whispering to each other. At the end of the pool, Maddy's office door was closed and the blinds were closed. They were never closed during practice. Maddy had always had an open door policy; any swimmer could talk to her at any time. Jessie frowned and climbed onto the bleachers beside Katie.

"What's going on?" she whispered to Katie.

"Jessie, you won't believe it!" Katie said. "Someone is trying to get swimmers to use steroids! In our own club. It's just like Calgary."

Jessie stared at Katie, unable to speak. "Do they know who it is?" she asked at last, forcing the words from her mouth. She wished she knew where Troy was; he hadn't been waiting for her in the lobby as he usually did.

Katie shook her head. "No. Maddy is calling everyone in one at a time, talking to all of us. She's pretty mad."

"Well, if they don't know who was offered the drugs, how do they know anything is going on? Who said something to Maddy?" Jessie asked, confused. Michael walked past as she finished speaking and Jessie felt cold suddenly. Before the thought could fully form in her mind, she pushed it away, turning around so she couldn't see Michael at all.

"I think Maddy found a letter or note or something. I'm not sure. I'm glad it wasn't me! I can answer her questions honestly," Katie said.

"Let's get going on a warm-up people," Darren called out, clapping his hands together. The little groups spread apart along the pool deck and the sound of splashing filled the air. Jessie glanced at the office one last time before she adjusted her goggles and headed for the pool.

"Jessie," Maddy called from behind her. Jessie stopped and turned slowly. "Could you come in the office, please?" her coach asked.

Jessie's heart pounded and her mouth was dry. She thought she might collapse, her legs felt so weak. "What's going on?" she asked, forcing herself to look at Maddy as she went into the office and closed the door behind her.

Maddy leaned against the counter and gazed steadily back at her. Her voice, when she spoke, was edged with a toughness Jessie had never heard before. "This morning, after practice, I found an envelope on my desk. The letter inside said that someone was offering anabolic steroids to some of the swimmers on my team. The letter writer didn't tell me whether or not anyone was actually using them. The letter writer didn't sign his or her name to the note either. They did, however, name the person he or she thought was pushing them. I don't like rumours, and the sneakiness of the whole business is making me sick to my stomach. There has been stuff floating around this club since September from various sources and I have decided it is time to put a stop to it. I probably should have said something a lot sooner," Maddy said, shaking her head. She stopped speaking for a second and just looked at Jessie.

"Has anyone approached you?" her coach asked at last.

"No one has asked me about taking steroids," Jessie said truthfully, a bad feeling creeping over her. She was pretty certain she knew who had been named in the note.

"What about Troy, Jess?" Maddy pushed.

Jessie's heart pounded even harder. "Troy wouldn't do that. He doesn't use drugs!" she cried, almost jumping from her chair. Her suspicion had been right.

"Easy," Maddy told her, placing a hand on Jessie's shoulder. "How do you know for sure that Troy doesn't use steroids, Jessie? After all, you haven't known him very long. He might not have told you about it."

Jessie took a deep breath, deciding, as she let it out slowly, that she had no choice but to tell Maddy everything. "I know because I asked him for them and he had a fit," she said honestly, looking at the floor. "He asked how I could think that he used drugs. He was so upset, I know he was telling the truth. He told me I didn't want to go there. He said he'd help me improve with hard work." The silence when she finished speaking was overwhelming, but not unexpected. She couldn't make herself look up and meet Maddy's shocked eyes. She stared at the floor until the tiles swam before her eyes.

"Why, Jessie? Why would you even consider such a thing?" Maddy asked, sounding so disappointed Jessie almost cried.

"When I came back from Christmas, something was missing," Jessie said. "I had no stamina, no strength. I couldn't get myself together. My shoulder hurt so much. Extra practice wasn't helping, the physio wasn't helping, nothing." She stopped and looked at her hands. Had it all been so cut and dry at the time? Her story, one long excuse really, seemed weak and contrived now. She cleared her throat.

"Troy said he could help. I thought," she paused for a second. "I thought he was talking about steroids. There were rumours in September when he first joined the club, you know the ones, and I thought maybe they were true after all. But he was talking about vitamins." She finished her story and sat waiting.

The silence was heavy. Jessie stared at her hands, folded tightly in her lap. She felt very exposed, sitting there in her bathing suit, with her hair tucked under her bathing cap. She could feel the tight elastic of her goggles still sitting on her forehead. It was so quiet in the little office, Jessie almost believed Maddy had left, but when she looked up, her coach was still leaning against the counter. The blinds were pulled, giving them privacy, but Jessie could picture the pool in her mind; the rolling expanse of blue water taking on a life of its own. She longed to be there.

"Thank goodness," Maddy said at last, her voice soft. "Thank goodness you asked someone who is clean. Thank goodness it isn't true," Maddy whispered, more to herself than to Jessie. She moved from the edge of the desk and sat heavily in the chair. It rolled a little as her weight hit it.

"The fact that you felt desperate enough to ask for drugs bothers me," she continued. Jessie looked at the floor again, anticipating the lecture she knew she deserved. "You are one of this team's best assets. You have a long, successful career ahead of you in competitive swimming and you almost threw it all away. I have an idea that you don't even really know what steroids do, right?" Maddy asked and Jessie could only shake her head. Maddy sighed.

"They make a woman more masculine, basically," she said. "Your voice deepens, you grow more body hair, you could develop a nasty temper. Some users get acne on their face, chest, and back. You might not be able to have children later, and there are a whole lot of other medical complications." Maddy was quiet for a moment, letting her words sink in. "I don't believe that any amount of speed or strength could make up for the loss of good health and a family one day."

"It was taking too long!" Jessie cried, jumping up. She wanted to run from the room, to escape the image Maddy had created in her mind. She almost hated her coach for putting it there.

"I thought you were smarter than that, Jessie. I thought you knew injuries and illness were facts of life in sport. We were working through your injury together and you were getting back to your old form," Maddy went on. "You were doing it! You were nearly there. Your times were only seconds off your Nationals times from last summer. You have unrealistic expectations for yourself, Jessie. I think they need adjusting. I'd like you to take a couple of days off."

"No!" Jessie cried, nearly lunging at Maddy.

"Today is Thursday," Maddy went on as though Jessie hadn't spoken at all. "Come back Monday morning. I want you to have a rest, some time to think. You're obsessed, Jess. Take a step back and regroup." Maddy stood up and walked to the door, allowing no argument, no negotiation. Jessie stood up, furious but powerless, and left the office.

14

Regrouping

When she got home, she escaped to her bedroom and hid there, not wanting to talk to anyone. Her mother glanced at her briefly as she flew up the stairs, but she didn't follow her. Jessie knew they wouldn't leave her alone forever. She wasn't surprised when, after dinner, there was a knock on the door and her mother and father came into the room. Jessie watched them from where she lay, curled in a ball on the bed, but she didn't move. Her father leaned against the door, her mother sat at the desk. For a long moment, the only sound was breathing and, from somewhere else in the house, the sound of water running.

"You came home from practice very early today, Jess," her mother said after a minute. "Did something happen?"

"Maddy sent me home."

"Are you going to tell us why?" Mr. Cameron asked calmly.

"She thinks I'm too obsessed with swimming and that I need to 'regroup.' I can't go back until Monday," Jessie said. She had a funny feeling they already knew why she was home, that Maddy had told her parents about their conversation.

"I see. Did something specific happen to make Maddy think this?"

Jessie sat up and glared at her mother. "You know what happened. Maddy told you everything."

"We'd really like to hear it from you, Jess," Mrs. Cameron told her.

Jessie swallowed hard then looked at her mother and then at her father. She told them everything, everything she had told Maddy and everything Maddy had said to her. When she was finished she felt drained of energy.

"I didn't take anything; I just asked Troy about them," Jessie said, throwing it out in the hope that it would soften their disappointment in her.

"You thought about taking them, Jessie, and that's almost as bad," Mr. Cameron said.

"I don't know if I even thought about taking them," Jessie said, sighing deeply. "Really, it was all just, just..." she started but didn't go on.

"Just what, Jessie?" Mrs. Cameron pushed.

"A mistake! It was a mistake, that's all. For a split second, I thought I could use them, get faster, then stop and it would help me. I just wanted to be faster, that's all."

Her father brushed a hand across his head, messing what little hair he had. Behind his glasses, his eyes were troubled. The silence was heavy, but Jessie didn't have the strength to break it. She could feel their disappointment and knew there was more to come. "Did we ask too much of you?" Mr. Cameron asked at last.

"No, never! It was always me. You guys have never pushed me," Jessie told them both.

"But maybe we should have been more aware of what was going on with you," her mother said, coming to sit beside Jessie on the bed. "You have always been so independent and confident. I have never felt like I have to watch over you, but maybe I should have been paying more attention," she went on, pulling Jessie close to her.

"I'll be okay, Mom, really," Jessie said, wishing she meant it. She was glad her mother was there beside her.

"I know you will, Jess," Mrs. Cameron agreed.

"You have some thinking to do in the next few days, though," Mr. Cameron said.

"I guess so," Jessie said and sighed. "But first I have some phone calls to make."

Her parents stood up. "We're a family, Jessie," her father said. "Let's work through this together, okay? There is no need for you to do it all by yourself." He winked at her and her parents left Jessie alone with her thoughts.

* * *

"I'm not sure I want to be bothered anymore, Jess," Troy told her over the phone, sounding defeated.

They had been over and over everything that had gone on that day. What Maddy had said to Troy, what she had said to Jessie. Jessie had told him about Maddy's reaction to her story and how she was taking a couple of days off from practice. Neither of them had mentioned what Jessie knew they were both thinking; who had planted the letter? Who had started the rumour?

"You can't give in to it, Troy! They'll win if you do," Jessie cried.

"How long am I supposed to keep proving myself innocent? It was supposed to be different here, but it's turning out to be Calgary all over again."

"What about me, Troy? I thought you were going to help me make it to the Nationals."

"Oh, Jess. I'm so sick of it all." Troy sighed heavily. "But I won't leave until you make Nationals, if I decide to go," he said at last, but Jessie found it cold comfort. "I'd better go.

I've got a bunch of stuff to do for school. I'll talk to you tomorrow, okay?" he said. "And Jess?"

"Yes?"

"Thank you for sticking up for me. I hope you know how much that means to me," Troy said.

"Yeah, I know. You're welcome." Jessie hung up and sat staring at the phone for a long time, thinking of Troy and also of the other call she had to make.

She had to force herself to dial Michael's number. Her fear that he was at the bottom of the whole mess wouldn't go away, even though she felt guilty even thinking such a thing of him.

"What happened to you at practice today, Jessie?" Michael asked almost immediately.

"I went home. I won't be there tomorrow either," she said, feeling as though she was talking to a stranger.

"Oh. Troy wasn't there either. This doesn't have anything to do with all the crap floating around about someone pushing steroids, does it?" Michael asked and Jessie felt her anger slip out of her control.

"Gee, Michael, I wonder? But you probably don't know anything about any of it, do you? Huh? These rumours just came from nowhere? From no one?" she snapped.

"Back off, Jessie. I didn't start any rumours. Don't go around accusing people without any proof," Michael told her shortly.

Jessie started to laugh; she felt almost hysterical. "Listen to you! You are such a hypocrite! What do you think you've been doing to Troy since he came to the club? You've thought he was taking steroids right from the beginning and nothing he or anyone else said to you has made you change your mind. You have never had any proof, just rumour and gossip. You've been jealous and mean the whole time and I'm sick of it." Jessie closed her eyes suddenly exhausted by everything.

"I have to go," she said and hung up without giving him a chance to say another word. Her friendship with Michael was as good as over, Troy was ready to quit swimming, and Jessie didn't even know if she wanted to continue swimming. Somehow none of it seemed worth it anymore.

She went to bed early, but she lay staring at the ceiling for a long time, unable to turn off her thoughts. In the morning she felt no better, just exhausted. Jamie looked at her in surprise when she headed off to school at eight o'clock, but he didn't ask and Jessie didn't offer any explanation. But Jamie was waiting for her at three, however, in his rattling, frightening old car. Jessie contemplated ignoring him, but it was damp and the sky was threatening more rain. She climbed in silently and sat staring out the front window as Jamie drove out of the parking lot.

"You going to tell me what happened, Jess?" he asked after they had driven a few blocks.

"Someone left a note on Maddy's desk saying Troy was offering steroids to some of the kids on the team. They didn't say who and they didn't sign it. Maddy wanted to know if I knew anything about it. I told her that Troy didn't do drugs and the reason I knew that was because I had asked him for some and he had flipped out on me. I cleared Troy, but I have managed to secure a two-day suspension to think about my swimming career and regroup."

"That's rough, Jess," Jamie said softly, glancing at her. "Things are that bad, eh?" he asked.

"Things are crap, Jamie." Jessie breathed deeply and hoped she wouldn't cry.

Jamie drove up to the house and pulled on the emergency brake. He turned sideways on the seat and looked at Jessie. "Does Troy appreciate what you did for him?" he asked and Jessie laughed weakly.

"Yeah, he does. He isn't sure he wants to stay with the team, though. He says he's tired of having to prove himself innocent to everyone all the time," Jessie said. "He told me all about Calgary and how everyone was blamed. There were a lot of rumours and gossip. A lot of guys' careers were ruined by it all. He decided to come out here to live with his dad, to start fresh, and now the same thing is happening here."

"I was one of them too, hey?" Jamie said and Jessie nodded. "Next time I see him I'll tell him I'm sorry, okay?"

"That would be nice, thanks. I just wish others would do the same thing."

"You gonna be okay, Jess?" Jamie asked, glancing at the cracked clock on the dashboard.

"Yeah, I'm fine. Really. Thanks for the ride," Jessie said with a small smile, then climbed out of the car.

The house was empty when she let herself in and she welcomed being alone. Her swim bag was still lying in the entrance where she had dropped it the day before. Jessie sat down on the steps and opened the bag, pulling things out of it. The familiar smell of chlorine wafted up. She pulled her bathing suit out and held it up, examining it. She would have to replace it soon. Chlorine ate the lycra so quickly. She went through at least three bathing suits in a season, sometimes four. Jessie put the suit on the step beside her and reached in again. Her goggles, two pairs, one for practice and one for racing, were safely confined to their plastic cases so they wouldn't be scratched. The huge turquoise towel, her name sewn in coloured fabric across the middle, was neatly folded. She set it beside her bathing suit. Her bathing cap, dusted with talcum powder so it wouldn't stick to itself, lay on the bottom, hidden beneath her towel. A small toilet bag held deodorant, shampoo, conditioner, and soap. One by one she pulled the other things out: old programs from swim meets, her paddles, and pull buoys, a ripped bathing cap, the jewellery box that had held Troy's bracelet.

She placed everything on the stairs and held the empty bag upside down, shaking it vigorously. Nothing but some small pieces of lint and hair drifted down to the floor and Jessie threw the bag across the tiled foyer, watching as it hit the closet doors and slid soundlessly to the floor. What had she been hoping to find? she wondered, staring at it. Answers? But there was nothing, nothing but the pile of things lying beside her. She sat with her arms wrapped around her knees, staring at the door, thinking.

15

Everything You Hear

J essie returned to the pool Monday morning. Her mother dropped her off, giving her hand a squeeze as Jessie climbed out of the car. She wasn't sure what to expect as she pushed through the changing room doors and joined the noisy mass of girls.

"What happened to you last week?" Katie asked, looking up as Jessie dropped her bag on the bench beside her.

"I took a couple of days off," Jessie explained, keeping her voice light.

"That's news," Tamara cracked. "Aren't you the one who was doing more work than the rest of us? What happened to all that?" she asked, but Jessie ignored her and continued changing.

"So, did Maddy tell you anything?" Katie asked as they walked out to the pool deck together a few minutes later. "Do you know anything about it? Who it was?"

Jessie dropped her bag on the bleachers and started stretching. "No, I don't know anything about it. I think someone made it all up," she said. She was thankful that Maddy hadn't told anyone else who was named in the note.

"You don't think it's true?" Katie asked, surprised.

"Well, do you know anyone who was asked? I don't." Jessie shrugged. "Someone obviously just wants to cause some trouble."

Katie stopped stretching. She stood in front of Jessie, playing with the strap of her goggles. "Some of the team think Troy was involved. I told them they were wrong, but a couple still think so."

"Troy was not involved. He doesn't take steroids and he doesn't sell them to other kids," Jessie told her, her voice hard and low. "If anyone else says that to you, you tell them that. You can ruin a person's whole swimming career by spreading lies like that." And they have, she thought.

"Hey, I'm on your side, Jess," Katie reminded her.

"Yeah, I know. Sorry," Jessie mumbled. "Let's get started, only two more weeks until the qualifying meet, right?" she said, forcing a smile.

"Hold up, girls," Maddy said, approaching them along the pool deck. Jessie and Katie looked at each other and slowly moved to the bleachers. "All of you, come and sit in the bleachers please. I have something to discuss with you."

* * *

"You will never guess what happened at practice today," Jessie said when Troy arrived at the door later that evening. She dragged him inside and down the stairs to the rec room.

"It was Cody Berenson," she announced when the door had been closed and they were sitting down. "He was jealous of your speed and wanted to get you kicked off the team. Maddy told us this afternoon that he won't be back to practice. She said she doesn't want athletes in her club who would deliberately try and hurt the reputation of another swimmer." She sat back in the chair and watched for Troy's reaction. He sat silently for a long time, just looking at her.

"I hardly even talked to the guy," he said at last, shaking his head. "What else did Maddy say?" he asked.

"She talked for a long time about gossip and spreading rumours about people. She asked us to think about how we would feel to have things that were untrue said about us. She also said that if even the hint of a rumour came to her ears, the person who spread it would be out of the club immediately. She was really choked. I think everyone got the message," Jessie said.

"I don't know, Jess," Troy said. "Just like that, everyone who thought I was using drugs is going to believe I'm not?"

Jessie leaned forward on the couch, shaking her head. "But Maddy told us it was Cody! He was jealous of you and wanted you to leave the club. He's been kicked off the team. Everyone heard Maddy say it. She told us you hadn't done anything wrong, the rumours were all false."

"Just because they heard it doesn't mean they believe it. We both know some people who don't want to believe I'm clean," Troy told her and shrugged. He leaned back, his face still troubled. "You don't know what it's been like, knowing people believe the stories they hear. Even though they have never had any proof or even any reason to think I was using steroids!"

Jessie sat back and looked at him. She knew he was thinking of Michael and even Jamie, although Jamie had talked to Troy and apologized. She couldn't really blame him for doubting things were okay. Michael hadn't said anything to Jessie at practice, hadn't even looked at her during Maddy's long lecture. She wished she could think of something that would make Troy feel better, make him return to practice but nothing came to her.

"Will you give it a chance? Please?" she whispered at last. "You promised you'd help me train for the meet and it's only two weeks away."

"Oh, Jess," he said, smiling a tired smile. "I'll stick it out through the rest of the season, through Nationals. I don't want to start in another club, not again. I don't want to leave you, either," he said, making Jessie blush.

"We're not quitters, right? Really, Troy," Jessie told him, "if you quit, you let Cody win. Even if he doesn't swim for us anymore, he wanted you gone. You have to stay, just to prove to all of them that you are a winner, that you don't give in."

"This has been a rough season for both of us, hasn't it?" Troy asked.

"It's not over yet," Jessie said with a smile.

16

Great Lengths

You ready for this, Jess?" Troy whispered to her as they pushed through the doors of the huge university pool complex. Jessie shuddered.

She couldn't believe how fast the weeks had gone by. The last qualifying meet of the season was due to begin in an hour; by the end of the weekend she would know whether all her hard work had paid off or not. It was frightening.

"I'd like to go home and back to bed, really," she muttered.

Troy laughed and grabbed her hand. "No, you wouldn't. You are going to be terrific, stupendous, amazing. Right?" he asked.

Jessie looked up at him and tried to smile. She had never been so nervous before a meet, not even at last year's Nationals. She wanted it to be over.

"I'll meet you on deck, okay?" Troy asked, leaning down to kiss her quickly. They separated and Jessie made her way through the crowd in the women's changing room to where Katie and Diane were already getting undressed.

"Morning, Jess," Katie said.

"I feel sick," Jessie told her, wishing the rolling in her stomach would stop.

Diane laughed and gave Jessie's shoulder a squeeze. "You'll be fine. I wonder where Tamara is? She's late," she said, looking around with a frown.

Jessie would not allow herself to think of anything but her first race. One event at a time, she kept telling herself. One event at a time until the end of the morning when they would swim the relay. She closed her eyes and breathed deeply. She wished her parents had listened to her and agreed to stay home, but no, they were coming and they were bringing both her brother and her sister. Jessie only hoped she didn't let everyone down, especially herself.

She didn't let anyone down, including herself. She made qualifying times in two of her first three events and placed in the top eight for the third, which meant she would swim it again in the final later that afternoon. Sitting in the bleachers with the others, dressed in her turquoise-and-white tracksuit, Jessie felt better than she had in months, more confident, stronger, more focused. She dared to believe that the worst was over.

"So, can your slump be considered officially over?" Troy asked, sitting beside her.

Jessie laughed, and threw her arms around him. "If you say it out loud, it might go away," she warned him, kissing his cheek. She was still hugging Troy when she looked up to see Michael standing beside them. Jessie dropped her arms immediately. Troy glanced at Michael, then at Jessie, and then he stood up and joined Jessie's parents at the top of the bleachers.

"Hey, Jess," Michael said in his old familiar way.

"What's up?" Jessie asked, suspiciously.

Michael flushed deeply and looked past her. He said nothing for a while, then he looked back to Jessie and cleared his throat. "May I sit down?" he asked, pointing to the space Troy had just left. Jessie moved over slightly, stunned that he was there at all.

"You're swimming better than I've ever seen you swim," he said. "All your extra work is paying off."

"Thank you," Jessie said shortly.

"I wanted to apologize," Michael said softly, looking at his bare feet. "I've been a real jerk for a while and I'm sorry."

Jessie's heart began to pound. "I'm not the only one you've been a jerk to," she reminded him.

"Maddy talked to me for a long time during all that rumour crap with Cody," Michael said in answer to her comment. "She knew I didn't like Troy and she also knows about our, you know, our run-ins. She basically told me to get my act together. Maddy also suggested I have a talk with Troy, iron things out."

Jessie felt a stirring of hope inside her but she stayed silent. She refused to make things easy for him. Beside her, Michael clenched his hands between his knees and stared at the ground for a long time. Jessie waited for him to go on. "You know how hard it was for you, having Tamara swim faster than you?" he asked, looking up at her. Jessie nodded. "Well, at least you had been sick. This guy is just faster than me."

"It was easier to believe Troy took steroids than admit he was a better swimmer than you," she finished for him. "That's pretty lousy, Michael. All of it is pretty lousy, really."

Michael looked at her and his blue eyes were glassy. "Yeah. It's been real lousy, Jess. Real lousy." He sighed. "I'm sorry."

"Why didn't you talk to me about it, before? Why'd you have to let it get so bad?" Jessie asked softly.

"You haven't been there for me much either, Jess," Michael told her. "All you've been interested in for months is swimming and Troy. I knew I came in third or even fourth, if you count Joanna. It didn't help anything knowing that you would always take Troy's side," he finished, holding out his hands in a gesture of helplessness.

"I guess I could try and keep things a bit more balanced from now on," Jessie promised.

They sat together silently for a long time and Jessie felt a return of their old easiness with each other. They still had lots to talk about, but it would all get said, eventually. She bumped against his shoulder and he smiled at her, a familiar, necessary sight.

"I thought I'd go have a talk with Troy, you know, before the relays start," Michael said casually, standing.

"Sounds like a good idea, really," Jessie agreed, and watched him climb up to where Troy was sitting.

* * *

Suddenly the only thing left to swim were the relays. Diane swam and Katie swam and then it was Jessie's turn. She climbed on the block, looking out over the vastness of the pool, mentally preparing for her four lengths. They were in fourth place. She could improve on that.

Jessie entered the water cleanly as Katie touched the wall, and surfaced, kicking hard. Stroke, stroke, stroke, breathe, stroke, stroke, stroke, breathe; the pattern played in her head like a mantra; smooth, smooth, smooth, relax, concentrate; stroke, stroke, stroke, breathe, stroke, stroke, stroke, breathe. Wall coming up, stroke, stroke, glide, legs flip, push hard like a spring; glide, glide, stroke, stroke, stroke, breathe … endless water, endless, endless, endless water; 100 metres of water to move through, to push past her.

She didn't let herself think about the three swimmers somewhere ahead of her. She didn't think of anything but her next stroke, her next breath. She swam the way she used to swim: hard. Then suddenly the last turn was coming up.

Jessie's shoulder began to ache as she spun around on the wall, pushing off one last time, but she ignored it. She wasn't the anchor, but she could swim as though she was. As anchor, she had always saved her very best for the last fifteen metres of the race. Only a few more strokes and she would touch the wall. Stroke … stroke … stroke … stroke … stroke … smack.

She felt the water rock as Tamara hit it but Jessie waited until she had pulled herself from the pool before she looked to see where they were swimming. She pulled her goggles off and scanned the pool. She quickly found Tamara, already touching the far wall for her first turn. Behind her came one, two, three, four, five … where were the other two swimmers? She squinted and found them, seconds ahead of Tamara. Jessie felt her heart sink a little. She hadn't pulled them into first, despite her efforts. Still, she reminded herself, third was okay. Tamara could still manage to win.

Jessie added her screams to Katie's and Diane's, cheering Tamara on, yelling until she had no strength left to yell. Slowly, slowly, Tamara pulled into second. She had only one length left to swim and Jessie crossed all her fingers and her toes. Tamara pounded through the final metres of her race and in the end she touched just ahead of the other girls.

The cheering was deafening as Jessie and the others pulled Tamara from the water, drawing her into the tight circle of their team. They had done it, Jessie thought, amazed. They had done it together.

* * *

It was after six when Jessie pushed through the doors of the University Aquatic Centre and walked out into the cool spring evening. She smiled to herself as she leaned against the wall to wait for Troy. She was exhausted but she could still feel the adrenalin pumping through her body from the day's events. It had been an incredible afternoon. She could still hear the cheers after they had won the relay. Plus, Jessie had qualified in all her events that day, including the relay. More importantly, she and Michael were friends again. Jessie smiled to herself, then closed her eyes and let her head rest against the bricks.

"Hey, Jess," Michael said, startling Jessie out of her doze.

"Michael! I thought you'd gone a long time ago," she said, blinking at him, confused. She moved away from the wall awkwardly, not sure where Troy was.

"Actually, I forgot something so Dad had to bring me back," Michael explained.

"Oh," Jessie replied, weakly. "Well, I guess I'll see you tomorrow then?"

Before Michael could answer her, Troy appeared at Jessie's side, his swim bag thrown over one shoulder. "Hi Michael," he said easily. "Good meet today, eh?"

"No kidding," Michael agreed, his voice friendly. "Pretty tough competition. Still, we all did okay, right?" he asked, smiling at Jessie.

Jessie nodded slowly. "Yeah, we did super," she said, staring at Michael.

"Well, gotta go, Dad's waiting. See ya 'round Jess. Bye Troy," Michael said and walked away, whistling. Jessie watched him go, amazed.

"Everything okay?" Troy asked, hugging her close to him. She looked up at him and nodded.

"Everything is great," Jessie said with a smile. "Just great."

Other books you'll enjoy in the Sports Stories series..

Baseball

☐ *Curve Ball* by John Danakas #1
Tom Poulos is looking forward to a summer of baseball in Toronto until his mother puts him on a plane to Winnipeg.

☐ *Baseball Crazy* by Martyn Godfrey #10
Rob Carter wins an all-expenses-paid chance to be batboy at the Blue Jays' spring training camp in Florida.

☐ *Shark Attack* by Judi Peers #25
The East City Sharks have a good chance of winning the county championship until their arch rivals get a tough new pitcher.

Basketball

☐ *Fast Break* by Michael Coldwell #8
Moving from Toronto to small-town Nova Scotia was rough, but when Jeff makes the school basketball team he thinks things are looking up.

☐ *Camp All-Star* by Michael Coldwell #12
In this insider's view of a basketball camp, Jeff Lang encounters some unexpected challenges.

☐ *Nothing but Net* by Michael Coldwell #18
The Cape Breton Grizzly Bears face an out-of-town basketball tournament they're sure to lose.

☐ *Slam Dunk* by Steven Barwin and Gabriel David Tick #23
In this sequel to *Roller Hockey Blues*, Mason Ashbury's basketball team adjusts to the arrival of some new players: girls.

Figure Skating

☐ *A Stroke of Luck* by Kathryn Ellis #6
Strange accidents are stalking one of the skaters at the Millwood Arena.

Gymnastics

☐ *The Perfect Gymnast* by Michele Martin Bossley #9
Abby's new friend has all the confidence she lacks, but she also has a serious problem that nobody but Abby seems to know about.

Ice hockey

☐ *Two Minutes for Roughing* by Joseph Romain #2
As a new player on a tough Toronto hockey team, Les must fight to fit in.

☐ *Hockey Night in Transcona* by John Danakas #7
Cody Powell gets promoted to the Transcona Sharks' first line, bumping out the coach's son who's not happy with the change.

☐ *Face Off* by Chris Forsyth #13
A talented hockey player finds himself competing with his best friend for a spot on a select team.

☐ *Hat Trick* by Jacqueline Guest #20
The only girl on an all-boys' hockey team works to earn the captain's respect and her mother's approval.

☐ *Hockey Heroes* by John Danakas #22
A left-winger on the thirteen-year-old Transcona Sharks adjusts to a new best friend and his mom's boyfriend.

☐ *Hockey Heatwave* by Chris Forsyth #27
In this sequel to *Face Off*, Zack and Mitch encounter some trouble when it looks like only one of them will make the select team at hockey camp.

Riding

☐ *A Way With Horses* by Peter McPhee #11
A young Alberta rider invited to study show jumping at a posh local riding school uncovers a secret.

☐ *Riding Scared* by Marion Crook #15
A reluctant new rider struggles to overcome her fear of horses.

☐ *Katie's Midnight Ride* by C.A. Forsyth #16
An ambitious barrel racer finds herself without a horse weeks
before her biggest rodeo.

☐ *Glory Ride* by Tamara L. Williams #21
Chloe Anderson fights memories of a tragic fall for a place on
the Ontario Young Riders' Team.

☐ *Cutting it Close* by Marion Crook #24
In this novel about barrel racing, a talented young rider finds her
horse is in trouble just as she is about to compete in an important
event.

Roller hockey
☐ *Roller Hockey Blues* by Steven Barwin and Gabriel David
Tick #17
Mason Ashbury faces a summer of boredom until he makes the
roller-hockey team.

Sailing
☐ *Sink or Swim* by William Pasnak #5
Dario can barely manage the dog paddle but thanks to his
mother he's spending the summer at a water sports camp.

Soccer
☐ *Lizzie's Soccer Showdown* by John Danakas #3
When Lizzie asks why the boys and girls can't play together, she
finds herself the new captain of the soccer team.

Swimming
☐ *Breathing Not Required* by Michele Martin Bossley #4
An eager synchronized swimmer works hard to be chosen for a
solo and almost loses her best friend in the process.

☐ *Water Fight!* by Michele Martin Bossley #14
Josie's perfect sister is driving her crazy but when she takes up
swimming — Josie's sport — it's too much to take.

I.S. 61 Library.